MW00849750

Readers love
ANDREW GREY

Rekindled Flame

"Definitely a well done and uplifting story."

—My Fiction Nook

"What a fantastic, multilayered, and emotionally moving book!"

—Rainbow Book Reviews

Fire and Snow

"*Fire and Snow* by Andrew Grey gave me exactly what I want out of a romance. It was an amazing *love* story…"

—Two Chicks Obsessed

Planting His Dream

"Andrew Grey gives us another good book about finding love and holding on to it despite tremendous odds."

—The Blogger Girls

Love Comes to Light

"…Andrew takes you on a journey of love and understanding of your limitations. You fall in love with all these characters."

—Alpha Book Club

More praise for ANDREW GREY

Eyes Only For Me

"A fascinating look deep into the hearts and minds of two men who never expected the discoveries they made along the way of changing and deepening their friendship to the point they become life partners."

—Rainbow Book Reviews

"This is a good story, with well written, well developed characters. There are some seriously hot steamy scenes, and deeply profound dialogue between the main characters…"

—*Divine Magazine*

The Gift

"Mr. Grey has given us a wonderful story of love and hope and I hope you each grab a copy and enjoy."

—House of Millar

Spirit Without Borders

"Nobody writes like Andrew Grey. I pick up one of his books and start reading, and I can't put it down. This one definitely was one of those books."

—Inked Rainbow Reviews

"The realistic picture Andrew paints about the conditions, the area, the lives of these people grips you and you become emotionally involved in the story and you won't want to put it down until you finish."

—Rainbow Gold Reviews

By Andrew Grey

Accompanied by a Waltz
Between Loathing and Love
Chasing the Dream
Crossing Divides
Dominant Chord
Dutch Treat
Eastern Cowboy
Eyes Only for Me
In Search of a Story
The Lone Rancher
North to the Future
One Good Deed
Path Not Taken
Planting His Dream
Rekindled Flame
Saving Faithless Creek
Shared Revelations
Stranded • Taken
Three Fates (Multiple Author
Anthology)
To Have, Hold, and Let Go
Turning the Page
Whipped Cream

HOLIDAY STORIES
Copping a Sweetest Day Feel
Cruise for Christmas
A Lion in Tails
Mariah the Christmas Moose
A Present in Swaddling Clothes
Simple Gifts
Snowbound in Nowhere
Stardust

ART
Legal Artistry • Artistic Appeal •
Artistic Pursuits • Legal Tender

BOTTLED UP
The Best Revenge
Bottled Up
Uncorked
An Unexpected Vintage

BRONCO'S BOYS
Inside Out • Upside Down •
Backward • Round and Round

THE BULLRIDERS
A Wild Ride • A Daring Ride • A
Courageous Ride

BY FIRE
Redemption by Fire
Strengthened by Fire
Burnished by Fire
Heat Under Fire

CARLISLE COPS
Fire and Water • Fire and Ice •
Fire and Rain • Fire and Snow

CHEMISTRY
Organic Chemistry
Biochemistry
Electrochemistry

Published by
DREAMSPINNER PRESS
www.dreamspinnerpress.com

By ANDREW GREY

GOOD FIGHT
The Good Fight • The Fight
Within • The Fight for Identity •
Takoda and Horse

LAS VEGAS ESCORTS
The Price • The Gift

LOVE MEANS…
Love Means… No Shame • Love
Means… Courage
Love Means… No Boundaries
Love Means… Freedom • Love
Means … No Fear
Love Means… Healing
Love Means… Family • Love
Means… Renewal • Love
Means… No Limits
Love Means… Patience • Love
Means… Endurance

SENSES
Love Comes Silently • Love
Comes in Darkness
Love Comes Home • Love
Comes Around
Love Comes Unheard • Love
Comes to Light

SEVEN DAYS
Seven Days • Unconditional
Love

STORIES FROM THE
RANGE
A Shared Range • A Troubled
Range • An Unsettled Range
A Foreign Range • An Isolated
Range • A Volatile Range • A
Chaotic Range

TALES FROM KANSAS
Dumped in Oz • Stuck in Oz •
Trapped in Oz

TASTE OF LOVE
A Taste of Love • A Serving of
Love • A Helping of Love
A Slice of Love

WITHOUT BORDERS
A Heart Without Borders • A
Spirit Without Borders

WORK OUT
Spot Me • Pump Me Up • Core
Training • Crunch Time
Positive Resistance • Personal
Training • Cardio Conditioning
Work Me Out (Anthology)

Published by
DREAMSPINNER PRESS
www.dreamspinnerpress.com

TURNING
the PAGE
ANDREW GREY

Published by
DREAMSPINNER PRESS

5032 Capital Circle SW, Suite 2, PMB# 279, Tallahassee, FL 32305-7886 USA
www.dreamspinnerpress.com

This is a work of fiction. Names, characters, places, and incidents either are the product of author imagination or are used fictitiously, and any resemblance to actual persons, living or dead, business establishments, events, or locales is entirely coincidental.

Turning the Page
© 2016 Andrew Grey.

Cover Art
© 2016 L.C. Chase.
http://www.lcchase.com
Cover content is for illustrative purposes only and any person depicted on the cover is a model.

All rights reserved. This book is licensed to the original purchaser only. Duplication or distribution via any means is illegal and a violation of international copyright law, subject to criminal prosecution and upon conviction, fines, and/or imprisonment. Any eBook format cannot be legally loaned or given to others. No part of this book may be reproduced or transmitted in any form or by any means, electronic or mechanical, including photocopying, recording, or by any information storage and retrieval system, without the written permission of the Publisher, except where permitted by law. To request permission and all other inquiries, contact Dreamspinner Press, 5032 Capital Circle SW, Suite 2, PMB# 279, Tallahassee, FL 32305-7886, USA, or www.dreamspinnerpress.com.

ISBN: 978-1-63477-586-1
Digital ISBN: 978-1-63477-587-8
Library of Congress Control Number: 2016906154
Published August 2016
v. 1.0

Printed in the United States of America

This paper meets the requirements of
ANSI/NISO Z39.48-1992 (Permanence of Paper).

To Dominic. I'm grateful he loves me and has a sense of humor. Somehow he always ends up as the model for the dead lover in my character's past.

Chapter 1

ROUTINE. THAT would be the word that best described Malcolm Webber—routine. His life had fallen into so many ruts he didn't even recognize them any longer. He got up on a Monday morning and shuffled his way into the bathroom. He didn't even crack his eyes open as he brushed his teeth, washed his hands and face, and combed his hair. There was no need. He knew where everything was because he went through the same motions each and every morning. The way Malcolm figured it, he could go through his zombie routine and it would be like getting an extra half hour of sleep. He'd already laid out his clothes the night before, so he pulled them on without thinking and left the bedroom.

The scent of coffee brought him to a kind of reality. He didn't smile, but the smell was a siren song with the promise that it would help wake him up and give him a little of the energy he needed to start his day. He descended the stairs, the coffee acting like the scent for a bloodhound. In the kitchen, Malcolm poured some into one of the mugs that sat next to the programmable pot and took his first sip. It was strong and sharp, just the way he liked it. He didn't turn on the television or make any unnecessary noise. His routine was too ingrained and practiced for that. He got some crackers, and a few bites of cheese from the refrigerator, and ate them for breakfast. Twenty years earlier, he and David had honeymooned in Europe after their commitment ceremony, and he'd gotten used to a more European breakfast. So ever since, he'd eaten a few crackers with cheese first thing in the morning. The action used to make him think of the little inn he and David had woken up in that first morning in Freiburg after hours and hours of travel. They'd stumbled downstairs after making morning love and had found a very different breakfast waiting for them than what they were used to. Malcolm had had cheese on some crisp type of crackers, and he'd had that same thing every morning for the rest of the trip. In the end, he'd brought the habit home with him.

Malcolm drank more of his coffee, the caffeine acting on his system, and he became more aware of his surroundings. He carried his mug through the house as he located his wallet and keys in their usual place and got his coat. It was frigid outside—winter in Milwaukee. But this was really cold. He felt it deep down, even inside the house. The air crackled around him, it was so dry. The air only felt like that when it was below zero outside. Not that Malcolm really thought about it. He knew the feeling, and his instincts had him grabbing his gloves and hat from their appropriate spot.

He set everything on the chair in the kitchen to finish his coffee. By now his eyes were open, but he still wasn't fully aware. His coffee hadn't really kicked in yet, but that would be just a few more minutes. The heated water that ran through the pipes that warmed the house *tink*ed every now and then as it reached a spot that was cool and the pipes expanded a little. Other than that the house was quiet.

Malcolm finished his coffee, rinsed the mug, and placed it in the sink. Then he walked through the house and up the stairs. He went back to the bedroom and pushed the door open, walking to the bed in the still-dark room.

He leaned over it and realized it was empty. In those few seconds, his morning routine came to an abrupt end. David was gone, and he wasn't coming back. Malcolm turned and sat on the edge of the bed. He'd actually made it to leaving the house thinking that David was still asleep in their bed. That he was still alive and with him. Malcolm sighed as tears welled in his eyes for the millionth time. For ten or fifteen precious minutes, at least as far as Malcolm was concerned, his David had been with him once more, and he hadn't felt the loss, his constant companion for the past thirteen months. He'd been free and happy, in a way, for a whole fifteen minutes.

Malcolm walked around to the other side the bed, his side, and straightened the covers. After more than a year, he still slept in the same space he had for twenty years. The other side was David's side of the bed, and he couldn't bring himself to use it. "Why did you have to go?" he asked the empty space David had occupied, but of course there was no answer.

Malcolm wiped his eyes with the back of his hand and left the tidied room, going back downstairs and pulling on his outside gear. He grabbed his case from near the back door and stepped out into air so cold it hit him like a hammer. He pulled the door closed and locked it before trudging along the snow-covered walk to the garage.

Inside the equally cold structure, Malcolm got into the blue BMW David had bought a couple of years ago and started the engine. He pressed the button to open the garage door and waited for it to lift while praying for the heat to come out of the vents. He pressed the button for his seat warmer and shivered for a few seconds until the door was up. Then he slowly backed out of the garage into the alley behind the house, closed the garage door, and cautiously moved forward, the tires crunching the snow loudly enough to be heard inside as he started the fifteen-minute drive into work.

The route to his office was familiar, and Malcolm usually made the trip on autopilot. But this morning the roads were covered with snow, and since it was so cold, patches of ice were possible anywhere, so he took some extra time.

"MORNING, MALCOLM," Jane said as he walked past her desk and into his office. "I put your coffee on your desk, along with your schedule for the day so far. It's Monday, and you know how Gary tends to change things up."

"Morning," he said, trying to at least sound cheerful. "Thanks for the coffee. I'm going to need it." He turned toward the door. "I wish Gary would make up his mind about what he wants to do. It would be nice to know what we're all walking into."

"You already have a busy client schedule, so you don't have much time today," Jane said.

That was the first good thing that had happened to him today. Gary Hanlan could call as many meetings as he liked to talk over whatever bee he had in his bonnet at that particular moment, but client appointments always took precedence. So at least his day would be somewhat predictable.

"You have half an hour to get ready."

Malcolm went into his office, booted up his computer, and got to work clearing his e-mail and reviewing the paperwork for his client appointments.

Everything was in his files and ready. He'd made sure of that, the way he always did. After all, he didn't get to be one of the best tax attorneys in the state by being disorganized and sloppy. Granted, taxation wasn't one of the glamour areas of the law. He wasn't a litigator, and he rarely handled any high-profile cases, like his colleagues often did. He did his work and regularly turned in as many or more billable hours than anyone else in the firm. His time was in demand, and he was good at his work. It wasn't particularly exciting, but then at his age, he wasn't interested in excitement or glamour. Making it through the days and weeks was about all he could manage at the moment, and that was just fine with him.

Malcolm was just answering his last e-mail when a knock sounded on his door. Jane opened it and ushered in his first appointment of the day.

GARY HAD broken his routine and not called any last-minute meetings, and by lunch Malcolm was still on schedule. Jane had gotten him his usual lunch—an egg salad sandwich on wheat toast with a small salad—and he ate it at his desk while clearing any new e-mails and inquiries.

"I got a call from a potential client. He says he needs some urgent help and was wondering if you might have an appointment available today," Jane said as she took a seat in the corner chair and flipped off her shoes. "I hate these things."

"Then don't wear them. You know I don't mind if you wear comfortable shoes in the office. It was Gary who had the ridiculous idea of what everyone should wear, and I voted against it. Yes, we need to look professional, but this isn't the fifties, and we're a law office, not a fashion house."

"But...."

Malcolm took a bite of his sandwich. "You wear what the hell you want, and if he gives you any grief, tell him to talk to me." He was getting a little tired of the power kick Gary was on, and it was time to make his opinion known.

"Thanks, Malcolm," she said.

He looked up from his screen and smiled at her. "You work for me, not him, and I want you to be comfortable." He leaned over his desk. "I can't stand wearing a tie. I know I have to because it's what clients expect, but I hate it. All summer long my neck sweats, and one of these days the copier is going to decide to eat my tie and the damn thing is going to hang me."

Jane rolled her eyes and took another dainty bite of her salad. "Please, you never make copies." She smirked, and Malcolm shook his head. "Now, if the coffee machine decided it wanted your tie, you'd be in trouble."

"Yeah. Couldn't you just see Gary coming in one morning and finding me dead in front of the coffee machine with my tie up inside?"

"Yeah. He'd probably have a fit that there was coffee on the floor and fire the maintenance guy," Jane said.

Malcolm laughed. It felt good for a few seconds, and then he went back to his computer. "Go ahead and schedule your caller in for the end of the day." It wasn't like he had anything he needed to be home for, and he could take an extra fifteen minutes to take a consultation.

"Okay," she agreed and sat back. "God, I love these chairs. The one I have out front is awful."

Malcolm paused in composing his e-mail and pushed away from his desk. "Get whatever chair you want. Consider it a birthday present. I have been trying to get the partners to upgrade some of the office furniture, but they aren't interested."

"I know. What we have looks fine, but they're starting to lose their support." She finished her salad and took the debris left from his lunch as she left the office, returning a few minutes later with another cup of coffee and a bottle of water. Malcolm knew the water was her way of saying that he drank too much coffee, and he probably did. So he opened the water and drank most of it before he started on his coffee.

He had a steady stream of clients that afternoon and ended the day with much more work than he'd started with. But he'd blocked out hours the following day to handle what he needed to, so he'd be all right. Sometimes he missed when he worked every waking hour of the day. He didn't need to do that much now, but it would give him something to fill the empty hours he spent alone.

"Your last appointment is here," Jane said, poking her head into his office.

"Thank you," Malcolm said as he made notes from his previous meeting and added them to the client file. "Please send them in and go home. I'll see you in the morning."

She checked her watch. "Are you sure?"

"Of course." He looked up at her as he stopped typing. "Why? If I know you, you've already finished your day's work and have my schedule for tomorrow set and ready to go." He glanced at the clock on his computer. "Just go and have a good evening." He wasn't going to quibble about half an hour. Jane stayed late plenty of times, and he liked that he could give her more time with her children.

"Thanks." She hurried away, and a man took her place in the doorway.

"Mr. Webber."

Malcolm put up his finger and went back to typing. He had to finish these notes or he'd forget some of the details. "Please take a seat. I just need a minute." He typed faster and got the last note down, then saved the file before closing it. "How can I help you?" He looked up from his screen and saw an impressive set of blue eyes staring back at him. They seemed to be David's eyes, and for a second he was confused. Hope shot through him, followed by a wave of unexpected grief. At the office he'd always been able to function, but not at that second. Malcolm blindly reached for his drawer and grabbed a tissue. He turned away and used it to cover his eyes. Shit, this couldn't happen now. The blue eyes weren't David's eyes because they weren't attached to David, but for a second his heart had leaped with hope that was, of course, futile.

"Are you all right?" the man asked in a deep, rich voice that helped knock Malcolm out of his thoughts. At least that was unlike David's mellow tenor.

"Yes. I'm sorry. Allergies," Malcolm croaked and wiped his eyes. He steadied his shaking hands and turned back to face his client. He sanitized his hands with the bottle he kept in his desk and then extended his hand after standing the way he should have when the man first entered. "Malcolm Webber. I'm sorry about earlier. I needed to get some notes typed quickly."

"Hans Erickson," the man said and took his hand firmly. "I appreciate you seeing me on such short notice."

Malcolm motioned to the chair, and Hans sat down again.

"What can I help you with?"

"I received a letter from the IRS stating that they believe I owe them a huge amount of money, and I don't understand it. I've paid my taxes and declared all my income for years." He picked up a thick file from next to him. "I wasn't sure what you'd want, but I brought the letter and the documents that came with it." He had a slight Scandinavian accent, not too heavy but pronounced enough that Malcolm wondered if he might have immigrated to this country.

"Let me take a look," Malcolm said. He accepted the letter and read it over, but it took longer than it should have because he kept looking at Hans. More than once the words on the page scrambled and blurred as his thoughts wandered to David, and then his attention returned to Hans and the way his shirt hung open, giving Malcolm just a peek at the blond hair showing in the V of his shirt.

"Well, it seems that the IRS is saying that you underpaid Social Security taxes in 2010 and 2011." Malcolm's mind began to scan through possible causes. "Do you have your tax forms?"

"I brought everything I had." He handed Malcolm a thick file with pages paper-clipped together.

Malcolm looked through until he found the years in question. It took him exactly five minutes to find the source of the issue. "You're a writer," Malcolm said. He thought he recognized the name from somewhere. "I read one of your books last year. I liked the action." Instantly he was transported back to the winter trip to St. Maarten he and David had taken together. David was in the water, darting through the waves, and Malcolm had sat huddled under an umbrella to stay out of the sun with a book. Hans's book. "It was really good."

"Thanks," Hans said with a bright smile.

"Did you do your own taxes?" Malcolm asked and was grateful when Hans shook his head.

"I had a tax guy do them. This is more than I can understand."

"Look here. He put your royalty income on the royalty line. But that's not for your kind of royalties. It's for mineral-rights payments and things like that. Book royalties should be handled as regular income. Because he did that, you didn't pay Social Security tax on that money." Malcolm did a quick check and found that after 2011, the taxes had been done correctly.

"What do we do?" Hans asked, biting his plump lower lip, and Malcolm swallowed hard as Hans's eyes filled with pleading and even relief. He'd seen those emotions in David's eyes so many times. Often in the bedroom, when Malcolm had him on the edge and all he needed was just a little more….

Malcolm pulled his thoughts back to the present and did some quick figuring. "You don't seem to have made much those years."

"No. I was just starting out and getting my first books published. It took some time for things to build," Hans said. "Those were fun years, though. The excitement of writing and then the first contracts. It was really heady."

"I bet," Malcolm said, trying to sound like he understood, but it was hard to remember feeling that way without David. There was only thirty thousand in income total, and Malcolm checked the statements. "Only about twelve thousand is subject to tax. So you owe about fifteen to eighteen hundred dollars." He picked up the notice and rolled his eyes. Of course they had added penalties and interest on top of interest and more penalties so it came out to over thirty thousand dollars. "What we'll do is file amended returns with the error corrected, and then I'll contact them and see if they'll waive the penalties and interest. That way you'll pay the missing taxes and it should be done."

"Do you really think they will?" Hans asked. "I've lost days of work time on the phone with them, and I got nowhere. They sent me round and round and basically told me to write a check and this would all go away. I don't have that kind of money to just write them a check over a mistake that my tax preparer made."

He sounded a little frantic. Malcolm understood. The IRS bureaucracy tended to do that to people.

"I understand. Did you contact your tax preparer?"

"He's moved on. I had an accountant do last year's taxes, and I'll use him going forward."

"All right. Let me work up an estimate of how much of my time this is going to take so you'll have an estimate of costs, and you can decide what you'd like to do." Malcolm folded his hands on his desk. "I always want my clients to know exactly what they're getting into."

"I appreciate that," Hans said. "Do you want me to leave all this with you?"

"That's fine." Malcolm pulled a blank file folder from his desk drawer and put everything he thought he was going to need into it. He really didn't think this would take very long, and it all depended on how soon he could get in touch with one of his contacts at the IRS. "I'll get the estimate out to you tomorrow, and once you approve it, we'll get moving." He had to turn away and take his time putting the file together to get his heart to stop beating in his ears. Hans was handsome, but those eyes…. Malcolm kept looking into those eyes, and thoughts he shouldn't be having sprang into his head.

Hans was a client, and Malcolm was not having… well, downright dirty thoughts about what was under Hans's tight shirt. No, those thoughts and images had no place in the office. Hell, they had no place in his life. David was gone, and that part of his life was over. He had accepted that months ago.

Malcolm stood and extended his hand, and Hans did the same. This time when they touched, a current passed through Malcolm's arm and down his spine, and he had to use all his self-control to keep from shivering. Hans's hand was warm, firm, and strong, with a hint of calluses on his fingers, probably from typing all the time. For a split second Malcolm wondered what those hands would feel like on him and then pushed it away.

"I'll walk you out," he managed to say as he released Hans's hand and opened the office door. Malcolm led Hans through the quieting office to the lobby and told him he'd be in touch.

Hans smiled and turned away. Malcolm had every intention of turning and going right back to his office. But his willpower failed him, and he turned just in time to catch a glimpse of Hans's backside in his designer jeans. The elevator doors opened and Hans stepped inside. Malcolm turned away before he could be seen and went back to his office.

He got to work, burying his attention in various tasks for his clients. He made notes of calls to be made and forms he needed Jane to fill out for him. After today he had a lot to do, and he needed to get organized in order to get it done.

"Working late, I see," Gary said after knocking once on his door.

"Long day without a break." Malcolm continued making notes, afraid he'd lose his train of thought. "I really need to get this finished." Part of the reason for working late was so that he could actually finish things up before going home. It certainly wasn't for chitchatting and wasting time. "Is it important?"

"I don't know," Gary said, drawing out his words, which always meant he had a bone to pick. "Do you have something against the standard dress code for the office?"

"I do. You're going overboard, and I won't enforce it." Malcolm sat back, now that he was done.

"I will."

"Not with my staff you won't," Malcolm said levelly. He wasn't going to argue about this. "Jane can wear whatever type of shoes she dang well pleases. This isn't a sweatshop, it's a place of business, and I want our associates and clients to feel welcome and comfortable, not like they walked back into the fifties. Jane always looks impeccable, and this dress code is ridiculous, so rework it and let everyone go back to the way things were."

"We need to present a proper image."

Malcolm stood. "You were elected senior partner to lead this firm. But you won't do that effectively if you go around solving problems that don't exist. I suggest you work on bringing in more clients and revenue. Look at who's producing what and work with the lowest producers to help them. That's what you should be doing, not worrying about dress codes and superficial things. Help to bring in high-profile clients. That's your job." Malcolm began gathering up his things for the evening. He liked to have his desk cleared and organized for the following day.

"I don't need a lecture," Gary said more loudly than necessary.

Malcolm walked over and closed the door. "You'll get one if you keep up this pissant stuff. Harlan was a master at bringing in new business for all of us. That's what you're being paid to do. You have the contacts, so get out and work them, find out what's shaking, and leave this office control stuff alone. This firm runs on the quality of our people, and every single person out there is the best at what they do. Don't make problems for yourself. That's all I'm saying." He softened his voice. "I wouldn't have voted for you if I didn't think you were up to the job."

"I guess…."

Malcolm smiled. "We all make mistakes. Put this behind you and get on to what's really important." He picked up his case and opened the office door. "I'll see you in the morning."

Gary followed him out and went quietly through to his corner office. Malcolm hated talking to him that way, but he'd tried a different approach before and gotten nowhere. He made a mental note to talk to Gary in the morning and make sure things were back where they should be.

He checked through the office area, noting those who were still working, meeting a few gazes, and then he turned and left.

Malcolm rode the elevator down to his car and stopped on the way home at one of his favorite restaurants for takeout. The man at the counter put in his usual order as soon as he saw him, and it was ready in a few minutes. Malcolm took his gyro and Greek salad home and ate in front of the television, then threw away the trash and put his feet up. He ended up dozing off for a while, read a little, and at ten o'clock he turned off the television, laid out his clothes for the morning, showered, brushed his teeth, and got into bed, sleeping on his side of the bed the way he always did.

It wasn't until after he got into bed that his routine changed. Normally he spent time thinking of David and their life together; it made him feel less alone. But tonight a pair of blue eyes, similar to David's and yet set in a very different face, kept running through his mind.

Malcolm rolled over after half an hour, punching his pillow. He needed to stop these thoughts. He alternated between chastising himself for having these thoughts about a client and feeling guilty for having them at all and somehow being unfaithful to David. He knew this was only his mind playing mean tricks on him because it had been a long time since he'd been intimate with anyone and he was lonely. He knew that. David had always been the outgoing one. He'd made friends easily, and he'd filled their lives and home with parties and warmth. Malcolm tried to keep up with their friends, but it wasn't his talent, and over the months, once the loss had worn off for most people, they had tended to drift away, and Malcolm couldn't blame them. The few times he'd tried to get together with people, he'd ended up either talking about David or standing aside and saying nothing because he wasn't sure what to say. In the end, he gave up on controlling his feelings and just let it go. There was no use trying to control his mind, and he eventually fell asleep remembering a beautiful pair of blue eyes.

Chapter 2

"HEY, BRO," his older brother, Peter, said the following day when Malcolm answered his phone during his lunch break, putting him on speakerphone so he could multitask. "Doing anything interesting?"

"I'm having lunch in my office with Jane."

"So no, then," Peter huffed. "Let me guess. Other than work, you've barely set foot outside the house in months."

"I have so," Malcolm said.

"The grocery store and gas station don't count, and neither does going to whatever store where you get your shirts and ties. I mean really going out and having fun."

"I try to tell him, but he doesn't listen to me either," Jane said loudly, and Malcolm shot her a dirty look. She shook her head and completely ignored him.

"I have to come to town next week on business and thought I'd fly in on Friday so we can have some fun this weekend. You need to get out, and I could use a few days of vacation."

"What does Susan think?"

"She says you need to get out more too, and she's going to her mother's for a few days with Anabelle." That explained a lot. Peter and his mother-in-law did not get along. They could keep from fighting and be civil for short periods of time, like at the holidays. But after a day all bets were off.

"Then come on. I don't know how much fun I'm going to be."

"Don't worry about that. I'll bring the fun, you stock up on some good wine. I'll fax over a list of possibilities."

"Of course you will."

"And make dinner reservations."

Malcolm rolled his eyes.

"You eat enough takeout and junk food. Doesn't your doctor have a fit? Listen, on Saturday I'll even cook if that will make you happy."

Malcolm's stomach rumbled happily at the thought. "It's a deal."

"I'll see you Friday."

Peter hung up, and Malcolm did the same, glaring at a smirking Jane.

"You called him, didn't you?" He stared bullets at his assistant. "When?" he asked in his best witness-intimidating tone.

"A couple of weeks ago. I was worried. You come to work and then go home. You aren't going out, and you aren't seeing friends. I bet you spend every evening either preparing documents or sitting at home, eating fast food in front of the television. Peter and my husband work for the same company, and I knew they were putting on this big conference, so I made a call to see if he was coming, and if he was, if he could get you out of that house for a few hours." She glared right back at him. "It'll do you good, and I wouldn't have called if I didn't care."

The touch of fear in Jane's voice gave Malcolm pause. "I know you do, but…."

Jane set her lunch aside on the table and came around behind Malcolm's desk. "You've stopped living since David passed. You work hard and smarter than you ever have, but then you go home and do nothing. The last party you went to was Harlan's farewell when he retired from the firm and stepped down as senior partner. I know you only came because of what he meant to you, and you stayed long enough to say good-bye to him and then left."

Malcolm was a man who'd worked in words his entire life. He wrote them, twisted and prodded them, used them against others when necessary, and yet at this moment they escaped him. He wasn't sure how to tell Jane that going to parties always reminded him of David. David had loved to throw parties and entertain, and he was the one who lit up a room just by walking in. He'd been the life of any party, and he'd always included Malcolm in his glow.

"I don't know, Jane. I just want some time to grieve and try to figure things out in my own way."

"But you're not."

"Yes, I am," Malcolm said.

Jane shook her head. "I've seen you outside work, remember? And I know you. You're going through the motions, and you need to think about starting to live again."

She placed her hands on his shoulders and began squeezing slowly. It felt good, and Malcolm closed his eyes. He hadn't realized how tense he was until some of it began to slip away.

"I'll get there, Jane. I promise you that. But right now I miss him so much, all the time." He was not going to cry in the office. He had shed plenty of tears for David before he was gone and enough to float a ship afterward. But none in the office, and he wasn't going to start now. "I'll be fine."

She stood and returned to her seat and her lunch. Malcolm stared down at his sandwich, appetite gone. He wasn't really looking at anything, and yet David stared at him in his mind. He was scolding him with that disarmingly charming expression of his that always told Malcolm he was being a butthead without saying a word.

"Okay. I'll try, Jane."

"Good. When your brother comes this weekend, let him take you out and have some fun. I don't care if you go bowling or to the movies, or even just take your brother to dinner. But go and have fun." She picked up her lunch and took a bite. "Oh, by the way, on a different note, we got the approved scope of services from Mr. Erickson. So you can do that magic you do so well."

"Great," Malcolm said and grabbed his sandwich for a bite. "I have the file here. I need you to prepare amended 2010 and 2011 returns. It's an easy one with one line of income that needs to be moved. Then we can calculate the Social Security tax difference, and I can get on the phone with the IRS and make them see sense." He handed Jane the file.

"What lit a fire under you all of a sudden?"

"Nothing," Malcolm said and returned to his lunch. "He's an author, and I've read a few of his books. They were good, and he seemed like a nice guy who took advice from the wrong person."

Jane took the files and peeked through them. "We tend to get that a lot."

"Yeah, we do. But in this case we can fix it."

"Okay. It's nice to see you excited about something."

"Jane," he said with a touch of warning.

"Well, he was certainly handsome enough. A big strapping man. He passed me as I was leaving, and he had an amazing smile."

She grinned at him expectantly, but Malcolm did his best to ignore it.

"You have to have noticed."

"Please, Jane. Just leave it alone. He's a client, and that isn't the way we talk about our clients." Malcolm began looking up the numbers he needed. "If you could get those forms completed right after lunch, we can probably get this one nailed up with a minimum of fuss." That all depended on how much grief Jane decided she was going to give him.

Thankfully she finished her lunch without more hounding, and he was able to eat again and then get back to work.

THE REST of the week was much the same—Malcolm worked, he stuck to his routine, and Jane gave him grief. On Friday, since Malcolm had everything buttoned up, he left the office a few hours early. He didn't have to pick up his brother at the airport because he was renting a car, so Malcolm went home and made sure the guest room was presentable and then did some last minute cleaning.

Peter arrived on time and blew inside like a whirlwind. "Malcolm." Peter was all smiles and energy, hugging him tightly before looking around. "Everything looks the same."

Malcolm shrugged and said nothing. Had he expected that Malcolm would have renovated or something?

"Am I in the guest room?"

"Of course."

"Then I'll get my things and you can change, and we'll go to dinner. I'm starved, and I know you have to be hungry. Have you lost weight?"

There had never been any doubt that they were brothers, with their tall frames and dark hair and eyes. They had the same angular face, but Pete had high cheekbones that gave him a movie-star look. Malcolm had always thought of himself as more ordinary. David had voiced a contrary opinion more than once. Malcolm had always felt as though he was the center of David's world, just like David had been the center of his.

"A little," Malcolm admitted. Not that he'd been trying, but he sometimes skipped meals. "Let me help you bring in your things." He needed to change the subject.

"I got it. There's no use both of us freezing half to death."

Peter went back out, and Malcolm notched up the heat a little. Then he met Peter at the door and led him upstairs to get settled.

"I made dinner reservations for tonight, and tomorrow I thought I'd cook," Peter said.

"It's good to have you here," Malcolm said.

Peter turned away from his luggage and hugged Malcolm once again. "I know this has been hell. You and David were, like, joined at the hip for years. You finished each other's sentences and completed each other and all that. But he's gone, and you need to move on with your life." Peter released him and stepped back. "Let go and have some fun. You're a single guy again." He did this weird dance that reminded Malcolm of a demented chicken.

"I don't want to be single, and please don't ever… ever do that dance again. There isn't enough brain bleach to get that image out of my head."

"Mal," Peter said in that tone that grated up Malcolm's spine. "I know you miss him, but David was the one who died, not you. It's been over a year. I know you needed time to mourn, but it's time you started living again. You don't have to date if you don't want to, but go out with friends. I know you haven't talked to

18

many people lately, but I'm sure they're all waiting for you to approach them again."

"I'm…." He was saying the same things over and over again and getting tired of it.

"You're a turtle. You've had your head pulled into your shell for too long. It's time to poke it back out and start to engage the world again."

"Nice analogy," Malcolm quipped. "How long have you been saving that?"

"Since Christmas, when you spent the entire day playing with Anabelle and pretty much ignoring everyone else. I had twenty people for dinner, and half of them didn't even know you were there."

That was a little extreme, but maybe Peter had a point. "Okay… so…."

"We're going out, so get changed into something that's more fun, less stodgy. Our reservation is for seven, but we can have a few drinks beforehand and maybe talk to some people."

Malcolm stifled a groan, but he turned and left to change. He found some casual clothes and a nice off-white and blue sweater David had bought for him years ago. It was an old friend, and it made him feel like David was holding him in a way. Yeah, he knew it was a little stupid, but he wasn't willing to let David go. They had spent too many years together—and they'd been through him working too much, misunderstandings, buying a home together… and so much else—for him to just let him go.

Once he was ready, Malcolm joined Peter downstairs and got their coats. It was going to get very cold, and Peter didn't have this kind of cold in Virginia, so Malcolm loaned him a heavier coat, not telling him that it had been David's, and they left the house.

The streetlights were already on, and a few stars shone in the sky. That meant it was going to get bitterly cold. They took Peter's rental since it was already warmed up, and Peter drove, with the aid of GPS, to the restaurant he'd chosen.

It was a trendy and loud Mexican restaurant. The bar was nearly full, and the tables were packed with small groups and couples eating and talking. The place smelled amazing, though, with peppers, spices, and even chocolate layering over each other. Malcolm's stomach rumbled, and he realized it had been quite a while since his hurried lunch.

"Grab that table there, and I'll check in with the hostess," Peter told him, and Malcolm threaded through the crowd and sat down. He turned to see where Peter was, and his view was blocked by a large man. He lifted his gaze and was greeted with a smile.

"I thought that was you."

"Hans," Malcolm said, tamping down the flutter in his belly and extending his hand to Hans. "How are you?"

"Much better thanks to you," Hans said with a grin as he held Malcolm's hand a little longer than was necessary. "I sent off the check with the revised paperwork, and I hope all that is behind me."

"It should be."

Peter approached and stood next to Hans.

"Hans, this is my brother, Peter. He's here in town for a few days. Hans Erickson."

"Your brother helped me with a tax issue."

"That's what Malcolm does." They shook hands. "What brings you here?" Peter asked.

"I was supposed to meet someone for a blind date, but that was half an hour ago, and it seems I've been stood up." Hans looked around the bar once again, and then his shoulders slumped. "Nothing like being dumped by someone you've never met before."

"There's an extra seat here. Come join us," Peter said as he pulled out the chair across the table.

Malcolm wasn't sure this was a good idea, but he wasn't going to counter Peter's invitation. Instead he nodded, and Hans sat down in the third chair.

"What do you do?"

"Hans is a writer of adventure stories. I've read some of his books." Malcolm smiled. In fact, he was feeling a little starstruck. He'd met a lot of people, but he'd never had drinks with a best-selling author before. It was kind of exciting.

20

Peter glanced at him and then back to Hans. "That's pretty cool. My reading is pretty much confined to food and wine."

"Peter works for a national wine and beer distributor. His interest has always been wine. I could tell you stories, but Peter would get huffy if I did." Malcolm grinned at Peter's growl. "See?"

Hans laughed warmly, and it disarmed Peter within seconds. That was amazing. Peter could be a force unto himself.

"Where are you from?"

"Virginia, outside Richmond."

"He and his wife, Susan, have the best daughter ever, Anabelle. She's incredible. She has her daddy wrapped around her little finger."

"She really does."

"What about you?" Hans asked, looking at Malcolm, whose throat chose that moment to close up.

"I was married for twenty years."

"Divorced?" Hans asked.

Malcolm shook his head. He could do this. "David passed away thirteen months ago after a battle with cancer." He breathed a sigh of relief. He'd actually been able to get the words out without falling to pieces.

Hans nodded, and Malcolm saw that same shadow in Hans's eyes that greeted him every time he looked in the mirror.

"My little brother." He put a hand over the floor to show his size. "He had leukemia. He fought for two years. He lasted until he was sixteen, so I know the ordeal that you went through. Cancer is evil, and it takes them away a little at a time. Up and down."

"Exactly," Malcolm said. "I took care of David at home as much as I could." He didn't want to think back to the day that David passed.

"Part of it is relief that they're not in pain anymore," Hans said. "Lars was hurting very badly by the end. You miss them, but seeing them that way…."

"Is that where the character of Markie came from in *Gathering Storm*?"

"Exactly, except in the story I gave him a happy ending because I couldn't bear to go through that all again. I wrote the story with the ending that I really wish had happened. It's one of the nice things about writing fiction—you get to have the ending you want."

Malcolm had rewritten the ending to David's story in his head more times than he could count. But of course it did him little good.

"Can I get you something from the bar?" the cocktail waitress asked as she placed napkins in front of each of them.

"I'll have a gin and tonic," Malcolm said, and Peter ordered a glass of some red wine he'd never heard of. Malcolm turned to Hans.

"Just a Coke, please," he answered, and the server hurried away. "I have to drive home."

"Malcolm is driving us home while I enjoy sampling the wine," Peter declared triumphantly. There was no use arguing. Malcolm rarely cared to drink that much, so Peter could enjoy his wine.

"Have you been in this country long?" Peter asked. "I only ask because of your accent."

"We returned after Lars died. My parents were Danish Americans, and my father was stationed in Denmark for a number of years. So I ended up learning Danish before I spoke English. I had dual citizenship until I turned eighteen, and then I had to choose. I wanted to be an American, and I was living here, so that's what I chose. The language issue sometimes trips me up, but I have excellent editors. I learned English when I was young, but it took some time to learn how Americans speak it."

The server returned and placed their drinks in front of them. Malcolm handed her his credit card, and she left with a smile.

"Did you always want to be a writer?" Peter asked.

"I don't really know. In school I hated writing themes and papers. But what I do isn't the same thing. My mother and father wanted me to be an engineer. I liked math, so I went to engineering school. I was good at it and learned fast. After I graduated, I got a job that I hated. It was designing roads, and that was boring. I got another job building bridges." Hans rolled his eyes. "I ended up working on the same bridge twelve times. One bridge design built in twelve places with minor changes. That was dull as dirt. My break from drudgery came when I got the chance to work on an offshore oil rig. My mother thought I was crazy, and my father said it would make a man out of me. They were both right."

Malcolm smiled. "I can imagine."

"Lots of work and then nothing but time and nowhere to go. I started writing stories to pass the time, and the ideas I started on the rig became the basis for my first book a few years later. I continued working and writing, fell in love, got married of a sort, split up, and kept writing through it all. Now I'm a forty-two-year-old author with an ex-husband, no children, and I'm trying to learn things all over again."

"How long were you together?" Malcolm asked, trying not to look surprised that Hans was gay. Granted, his gaydar was way beyond rusty.

"Fifteen years. I caught Troy sleeping with a friend of ours. Turned out that was his hobby—sleeping with our friends. He'd been doing it for years, and no one said a thing. I was the laughingstock of everyone I knew. So I dumped him and thanked God we never got legally married."

"Damn," Peter said. "What about your friends?"

"I dropped them too and started over. We sold the house, and I bought my own place and began rebuilding." Hans paused and drank most of his soda. "Sorry for laying that on you."

"Sometimes it's easier to talk to strangers," Peter said, then sipped from his graceful wine glass.

"Or my lawyer," Hans clarified, and Malcolm took a drink from his glass.

"Gentlemen, your table is ready," the hostess said.

"Would you like to join us?" Peter asked Hans and turned to the hostess. "Is that a problem?"

"No," she answered, and it seemed that Hans was going to join them for dinner.

That was Peter—he made friends everywhere and was incredibly sociable. It was something Malcolm had always been a little jealous of. Growing up, Peter had always been surrounded by huge groups of friends while Malcolm struggled. He'd always told himself it was because he was smart, but Malcolm now thought himself rather shy by nature. Or maybe he really was a dweeb like the kids had said.

"I don't want to intrude," Hans said, standing back.

"You're not. I was trying to get my hermit brother here to go out and talk to people rather than sit home and eat takeout and frozen dinners in front of the television. So having you join us is great." Peter swept them forward in a wave of energy.

"Please," Malcolm said to let Hans go first, and even though he knew he shouldn't, he couldn't help taking a peek at his backside. If it were possible, Malcolm would have done one of those bulging-eye things from Bugs Bunny. Either Hans's jeans were sculpted or the ass inside them was. Either way, the sight was a thing of beauty: high, firm, and bubbly. In other words, perfection. Malcolm didn't have time to think much about what he was seeing other than to wonder if Hans had been doing squats since the age of fourteen.

They reached their table, and Hans took a seat, hiding the object of Malcolm's fascination, and when Malcolm pulled out his own chair, he saw Peter flash him a look. Malcolm pretended he hadn't seen it and put on his best innocent face. He was good at that. It had come in handy the few times he'd been in court or when he was explaining things during an IRS audit. Nonetheless, Peter had seen and kept looking between him and Hans like some yenta from *Fiddler*. Malcolm had been busted.

"Are you working on a book now?" Malcolm asked to renew the conversation.

"Always," Hans answered. "I have one that's being readied for publication and another that I'm finishing up. I have ideas for the follow-up, but I have to see if they pan out once this one is done. In a week or so, I get to write the climactic scene. I know what it's going to be and how the bad guys are going to get beaten, but there's always some surprise for me that makes that part of the book really exciting. It's also the part where I discover if I forgot some scene or made a mistake that will take me weeks to go back and fix. After that it's the wrap-up and another story is done."

The server interrupted them as she talked about the menu and then gave them a few minutes to look things over. Malcolm was starving and chose quickly, with an appetizer he hoped would arrive soon. He was starting to feel a little light-headed and shaky, which he knew was the result of a lack of food in his system. The others seemed to have decided as well, and when the server returned, they all placed their orders.

"Do you like being a lawyer?" Hans asked as he turned his gaze to Malcolm, who found himself at a loss for words for a second.

Dang, Hans's eyes were incredible, and they reminded him so much of David. Not the rest of his face, just the eyes.

"Yes," Malcolm finally answered. "It's what I wanted to be since I was a kid watching *Perry Mason* and *L.A. Law* on television. I knew that reality wasn't depicted on those shows, but I didn't care. Of course, I found out that practicing law is very different from how it's made to look on television." He finished his drink and switched to water.

"Why tax law?"

"I fell into that," Malcolm said. "The firm I started out with isn't the one I work for now. It was in a small town where Peter and I grew up, in lower Michigan. Everyone pretty much did everything, but we got a raft of tax issues after a set of IRS rule changes, and the partners funneled those to me. I had to study the various rulings and cases as well as work through the bureaucracy involved. I met people, built up contacts, and soon I was handling the cases with ease. Over time I learned more and more, went back to school for an accounting degree and a master's in taxation law, and here I am."

"Malcolm is pretty brilliant," Peter said. "He took on the IRS a few years ago. Actually took them to court and won."

"They had set up a rule that my client at the time thought was against the statutes, and we were able to prove it. The IRS had to change their rules."

"Does that happen often?" Hans asked.

"No." That was one of his main claims to fame. Winning a case against the IRS was pretty big, and it meant that a lot of people wanted his help. "I was already a partner in the firm at that time, but it raised the firm's stature, and that's always a good thing."

The server brought the appetizers, and the conversation quieted as they all began to eat. After a few bites, Malcolm felt better, and he found himself looking at Hans more than he should—and dang it if Peter didn't catch him at it. Malcolm didn't want him to get the wrong idea, and knowing Peter, he'd have him and Hans married off and happily living together in minutes. Either that or he'd be just plain insufferable the entire rest of the weekend, saying that he'd been right.

"What was it like growing up in Denmark?" Peter asked.

"I guess it was different from most people there in that I was of American parents, but it was a happy experience," Hans said. "Being taught in a different language is a unique experience. By the time I entered school, I spoke Danish and English, and I had classes conducted in both. It was a very broadening experience for me, and I like to think it helped give me my love of words and language. We all think that the way we speak is the way everyone speaks and that everyone thinks the way we do, but it isn't like that. In Hawaiian there is no word for weather because it wasn't necessary. All languages are like that. What's easy to say in one takes a lot more effort in another."

Hans's eyes danced, and he bounced a little in his chair. It was amazing seeing such a large man move like that. For a few seconds, Hans was childlike and full of wonder. Malcolm tried to remember the last time he'd felt that way, and when he did, a cloud settled over him and he had to work to push it away.

They finished their appetizers, and the server took the plates and brought the main courses, which smelled divine and tasted even better. Malcolm ate with relish, savoring the heat of the peppers and snap from the spices and lime. The beef was sublime, and he finished it off without paying much attention to what was around him.

"Is he always like that?" Hans asked, pulling Malcolm out of his food haze. "You know you were making sex noises."

Malcolm colored, and Peter set down his fork, laughing. "That was something I don't think I want to hear about. I love my brother, but I do not under any circumstances want to hear about his sex noises… or sex in any way."

"Peter has a problem with anything squicky," Malcolm told Hans.

"That's a new one. Squicky?" Hans asked.

"See, to him gay sex is squicky, and he knows I'm gay but never wants to hear about the squicky parts. Just like I don't want to hear about him and Susan. Squicky. Though Peter's definition of squicky is pretty broad."

Hans leaned closer. "Even normal stuff?"

"Yeah. His squicky factor is pretty low."

"Good to know," Hans said with a wink. "I bet yours isn't."

Malcolm swallowed as Hans went back to eating. He was suddenly warm, and when he looked over at Peter, he found him with his head down, examining everything on his plate as though it contained the secrets of the universe.

Hans had been flirting with him. Malcolm was sure of it, and maybe he'd been flirting back. He wasn't really sure, but there was a tinge of excitement and energy he hadn't felt for years. Malcolm refused to examine it, because if he did, he knew it would lead right back to David, and that wouldn't help him at this moment. Malcolm returned to his dinner, cheeks heating. He shouldn't be flirting with anyone. David was gone, but Malcolm still loved him, and flirting with anyone after…. It was just wrong. He put his foot down on his own thoughts and concentrated on what he was doing at that moment.

"Aren't they cute?" Peter asked, and Malcolm followed his gaze to where two men sat. "As long as I don't have to hear the details I'm fine."

They were about twenty and looked very young as they gazed a little nervously at each other. It was obvious to Malcolm that they were together and out on a date.

"I barely remember being that young," Malcolm said softly. It didn't take long for him to recall those first heady dates with David, the excitement and zing of each touch, how his uncertainty added to the energy of nerves firing all at once, how each gesture seemed meaningful.

Malcolm blinked a few times and then stood and excused himself. He turned and went back out front to the restrooms, then ducked inside. He was alone, and he grabbed a tissue and pressed it to his eyes. All he kept thinking about was David. He knew he shouldn't. It had been long enough, and everyone was right. Maybe it was too soon to date, but it certainly wasn't too soon to start living a little again. Everything seemed so hard, and yet here he was out with Peter and having dinner with Hans. In a strange way, he knew he could make it through. He'd been having a good time until he let his memories get the better of him.

Malcolm wiped his eyes and splashed some water on his face, dried it, and then checked in the mirror to make sure he didn't look like a jilted bride before leaving the bathroom and returning to the table. He sat back down and finished his meal, letting Hans and Peter talk.

"Would you gentlemen like some dessert?" the server asked as she cleared the plates.

Peter ordered the chocolate cake, so Malcolm and Hans followed suit because, well, it was chocolate. She brought three pieces, and as soon as Malcolm put a forkful into his mouth, he entered another dimension of taste. They had added chilies, just enough that the chocolate exploded and then morphed into a touch of heat before the bite disappeared. It was incredible, and each bite acted a little differently, some with more heat and others with more chocolate. What an unbelievable treat.

"You're doing it again," Hans said very quietly to him with a warm smile that might have held a tentative invitation.

Malcolm wasn't completely sure, and those kinds of invitations weren't the kind he'd be accepting at the moment. Though something did happen: Malcolm felt a spike of heat and desire rise from down deep in a way he'd never expected to again. The way Hans looked at him, with heat and maybe desire, made a part of him he thought was lost come to the front. Interest, real interest in another person, was something he had written off as being too old for, and after David, he'd put that part of his life on a shelf.

"I'm sorry," Malcolm whispered.

"Don't be. It's nice."

Hans might have winked again, and thankfully Peter seemed unaware of the interaction. Malcolm finished his dessert and managed to keep quiet, though it was difficult. When the server came back with the check, he paid it gladly.

"Do you have plans for the rest of the evening?" Peter asked Hans.

"I was going to go get some more work done. This amazing meal and your company have helped settle a scene I've been having trouble with, and I want to get home before I lose what I need to get written. But thank you for dinner." Hans turned and flashed Malcolm a huge smile. "That wasn't necessary and was so very nice."

They stood, and Malcolm shook hands with Hans. Peter did the same, and Malcolm excused himself, taking a minute to go to the restroom before he bundled up for the cold.

When he returned, Hans had left, and Malcolm put on his winter gear before accepting Peter's keys. They returned to the rental car, and Malcolm pointed the car toward home.

"I was thinking we could go out for a while," Peter said.

"Where?" Malcolm asked. "I know you think I should go meet people, but I'm not a kid again, and trolling the places we did before we met our partners just isn't in the cards. I have no interest in going to a bar or a club."

"Is that what you thought?" Peter asked. "I was thinking maybe a movie or… I don't know."

Malcolm checked the clock. "It's a little late for most shows. We could go home and see what's on demand. It'll be warmer."

Peter agreed, and Malcolm continued driving. By the time he reached the house, the temperature on the dash of the car read eight degrees, and it was going to get even colder. Peter jumped out of the car and raced to the door, doing what looked like a peepee dance until Malcolm caught up to him and unlocked the door.

"Jesus."

"It gets this cold a lot in the winter, though tonight is going to be one of the coldest." Malcolm hung up the coats. "Go on into the living room and turn on the television." He bumped the heat up a notch. Then he made some decaf coffee and joined Peter, who was huddled on the sofa under the throw.

Malcolm let Peter choose the movie, which could have been a disaster. Peter initially hovered over *The Imitation Game*, and Malcolm wasn't sure he could watch the end. The last time he'd watched it, the scene with young Alan waiting for his friend to come back to school with the coded love note only to have him not return had sent Malcolm racing to the bathroom. However, it seemed Peter was in a comic-book mood, and they ended up watching *Iron Man*.

"Hans was nice," Peter said as the movie queued up.

"Yes." Malcolm poured a cup of coffee and sipped the hot liquid.

"I think he likes you." Peter looked as though he might be teasing him. "Are you going to call him?"

"For what?"

Peter leaned forward and lightly smacked Malcolm on the back of the head. "A date. What else? I saw him winking at you. The man was flirting, and once I thought you might have been flirting back. Not that you're anywhere as smooth as I can be."

"Yeah, right. Go ahead and flirt. Susan would have your nuts for lunch if you flirted with women."

"Doesn't mean I don't still got it."

"What you got is rustier than a cemetery gate," Malcolm crowed. "Besides, how do you know he's interested like that? Maybe Hans was being nice."

"Please. You're one to talk." Peter reached into his pocket and pulled out a napkin, then pressed it into Malcolm's hand. "I got his number for you. If he wasn't interested, he would have said so instead of asking the bartender for a pen and giving me the number." Peter stood and made a slam-dunk motion.

"Sit down and watch the movie."

"Fine, but not until you answer my question. Are you going to call him?"

Malcolm groaned and turned toward the television. "Just watch the movie."

"You know I'm not going to let this go, Mal. He was really nice, handsome if you like that sort of thing."

Which Malcolm certainly did. Hans was the entire physical package for him if Malcolm was honest.

"And to top it off, he was definitely interested."

"Will you leave me alone?" He tried to sound angry, but Peter knew him too well.

"I don't want you to be alone for the rest of your life, and if things were left up to you, that's what would happen. You'd go to work and stay in your house, mourning David. Now you may be a queen sometimes, but acting like Queen Victoria is not going to happen."

"Where did you learn about that?" Malcolm was surprised David knew who Queen Victoria was. He'd never figured Peter for a history buff. Then it hit him. "Let me guess. Susan made you watch a movie about her."

Peter mumbled something, and Malcolm turned to stare at him.

"I pissed her off, and she said she'd cut me off for a week if I didn't. God, that thing was long and boring, and you are forbidden from ever becoming like that. So…." Peter leaned forward. "Are you going to call him?"

"You're like a broken record."

"Dude. I'll make a deal with you. I'll stop harping on it if you agree to call him and ask him out."

"Is this high school?" It sure as hell was starting to feel like it. "I'm fifty-two years old, not fifteen."

"I don't care how old you are."

Malcolm swallowed. "I saw his birthdate when I was reviewing his updated tax forms."

"So you looked?" Peter asked with a self-satisfied grin.

"That's ten years."

"At your age it doesn't matter. You're a guy and you still like guys, I hope, because there are few things you can count on in this world, and my big brother being gay is one of them."

When Malcolm rolled his eyes and nodded, Peter continued.

"Okay, then. You like guys, he likes guys, and he flirted with you. Also, and here's a big qualification, he's not dead, and neither are you. So…."

Peter crossed his arms over his chest, cocked his eyebrow, and waited. Malcolm did the same and stared right back at him. They used to do this for hours until one of them flinched.

"I'm a lawyer. I can do this all day."

"Call… him," Peter snapped.

"Fine," Malcolm said, and Peter started the damned movie already.

Chapter 3

PETER STAYED until after dinner Sunday evening, which he cooked again, thankfully—coq au vin that was heavenly. His conference was on the west side of the city, near Malcolm's office, and they had booked everyone into a hotel because apparently the activities would continue into the evenings. "A bunch of team-building stuff."

"Good Lord."

"Yeah. The last time we did something like this, they sent us all to a cooking thing. I don't think they thought I was being a team player when I explained the flaws in their recipes to them. Though I did save the day when I brought out the wine."

"Do you know what it is?" Malcolm asked.

Peter shook his head and then hugged him. "You take it easy, and if I can skate out early, I'll stop by to see you on my way out of town." He stepped back and picked up his bag. "I know I was giving you a bunch of crap, but give Hans a call."

Malcolm had hoped Peter had forgotten all about that since it hadn't been mentioned again in the past two days.

"Mal-colm," Peter groaned in that nagging way brothers had. "You promised you'd call him. Don't make me call you every day to hound you, because you know I will."

Peter's laugh reminded Malcolm a little of Jack Nicholson's Joker as he pulled open the door and stepped out of the house.

Malcolm watched Peter leave through the storm door. He closed the heavy front door once Peter was in the car, and when Peter was gone, he turned out the lights and settled in the living room in front of the television.

That night, Malcolm went to bed and slipped into his nightly routine without a thought. When he got up the following morning, he went back through his routine and left for work, barely registering what he was doing until he was in the car, when he pulled out into the snow and tried to come to a stop, only to have the wheel wrenched out of his hand as the tires moved it in the other direction. The car wasn't the only thing caught in a rut, and his was deepening each and every day.

Maybe everyone else was right. They'd seen that he wasn't moving on, and he had said he wanted more time, but all he'd really been doing was hiding. He'd become very good at that. A beep from behind him brought Malcolm back to his senses. Malcolm pulled forward and drove the rest of the way to work.

"You're a little late," Jane commented when he got to his office and set his bag down before slumping into his chair. "Rough weekend?" She placed his schedule in front of him and set his mug on the desk. "Thankfully it's quiet on the work front and your day isn't too heavy."

"Yes." He booted up his computer and reviewed his inbox. "Am I grieving too long?"

Jane stepped back. "I don't think so. Now, if you said you wanted to have some grand torrid affair with a much younger man, I'd probably pat you on the back and say to go for it. Lord knows you can afford it." She giggled. "But it might be too early for you to fall in love again, because you're not ready."

"That's what I tried to tell my brother."

"But there's nothing that says you can't go out, meet a few people, get together with friends, and stop moping. That stage might have gone on too long."

"Why does everyone want me to stop loving David?" Malcolm asked.

"We don't. No one does." She turned and closed the door quickly, which Malcolm appreciated. "But you didn't die with him. You'll always love him. That will never change, but start living again. I think David would want that."

Damn it, Malcolm knew she was right, but it still hurt so damn much, deep down, like a physical longing that could never be quenched. "I don't know if I can."

"Of course you can. You came back to work, and you've done fine. Go out with friends, and make some new ones if you want. You don't need to fall in love again, if that's what you're worried about."

Malcolm shifted his gaze to her from where he'd been watching the chair behind her.

"That's it, isn't it?" Jane asked.

"I had dinner with my brother on Friday, and Hans Erickson joined us. He flirted with me. Apparently Peter saw it and now thinks I should call him and ask him out. He made me promise."

"You had dinner with him?"

"Yes, and he apparently gave his phone number to Peter for me so it wouldn't be like I was using work records inappropriately."

"Have you called him?" Jane asked.

Malcolm shook his head. "I don't know if I'm ready."

"But you like him. I saw the two of you together. Mr. Erickson is a nice man, and he's an author whose work you really like. So call him, see if he wants to get together and talk books. There doesn't have to be anything romantic if you don't want there to be."

And there lay the problem. He'd already been around Hans three times—when they first met, a few days later when he returned to the office to sign his papers and send in the check to the IRS, and then at dinner with his brother—and all three times Malcolm's heart had beat a little faster, and he'd had to wipe his hands to keep them from feeling sweaty. Every time that happened, it felt as though his body was betraying him and that he was being unfaithful to David. Of course nothing physical had actually happened between them, but the idea that it could, that part of him wanted something like that, sent the rest of him into a well of guilt.

"I don't know what I want there to be, if anything."

Jane sighed softly. "Sweetheart. David passed away, but you didn't. I know you loved him, and so did he. If David is looking down on you or is acting as your guardian angel, he's rooting for you to move on with your life. Do it in whatever way you're comfortable, but do it." She patted his shoulder, and they stood quietly for a few moments. "I hate to break this up, but your first appointment is in five minutes, and then you have a break for a few hours."

"Thanks." She turned and left his office while Malcolm returned to his work and tried to put his game face on.

He had his consultation and accepted another client with a tax issue. This one was more challenging than Hans's, but nothing he couldn't handle. After he'd shaken his new client's hand and he'd left the office, Gary knocked on his door frame and stepped inside. Malcolm stifled a groan when he saw his expression.

"I was thinking this weekend that we should create a television commercial for the law firm," Gary said. "Something tasteful that highlights our strengths and explains the kind of things we do."

Malcolm stifled an overwhelming urge to roll his eyes. "Why is that a good idea?" he asked as gently as possible.

"It's a way to bring in a lot of new clients."

Of course. Malcolm had told him it was his job to bring in new clients, so rather than do the legwork, he'd thought of ways to try to make the clients come to them.

"Have you seen the type of firms that advertise? They mostly handle personal injury, malpractice, and other specific types of cases, and they make their firms seem like the legal version of a used-car lot." Malcolm motioned for Gary to close the door.

"I think it's a great idea," Gary said, "and this afternoon at the partners' meeting, I'm going to raise it before the rest of the partners. It would be tasteful and businesslike." He was as serious as a heart attack. "I only wanted to do you the courtesy of telling you before the meeting." Gary reached for the door, yanked it open, and strode out of his office.

Malcolm got up and walked to his open door.

Jane turned away from where she'd been watching Gary disappear into his office, and the entire office jumped when his door sharply slammed closed. She then turned to him, silently asking what happened, and shook her head. "Call him," she mouthed.

"Gary?" he asked softly.

Jane's expression changed to that look she gave him whenever he was being totally obtuse. Malcolm retreated into his office and pulled the napkin out of his pocket. He sat at his desk and dialed the number before he lost his nerve. When Hans answered, Malcolm said, "Hans, it's Malcolm Webber. I hope I'm not disturbing your writing or anything."

"No. I've already been working, and I'm just making breakfast."

"I had a nice time at dinner the other night, and I was wondering if you might want to…. I have a charity event on Friday. It's for the leukemia society, and the firm has purchased a table. I was wondering if you'd like to go with me." Malcolm felt as though he was about three seconds from losing what little was in his stomach. He wasn't sure why he felt like a teenager… and not in a good way. He hadn't been this nervous the first time he'd asked David to dinner. Maybe it was because of the pressure everyone was putting on him. At least once this was over, he could go back to a more comfortable life, and his brother—and Jane, and everyone else—could leave him alone.

"That would be nice," Hans answered, but Malcolm was so far in his head he almost missed it.

"Great. I can get your address, and I'll pick you up at seven. The dress is formal." God, he should have made sure Hans had a tuxedo.

"All right," Hans said easily, and Malcolm relaxed slightly. This could be fine. "It sounds like it could be fun," Hans continued, "and the cause is near and dear to my heart. I'll look forward to seeing you on Friday."

"Great," Malcolm said. "See you then." He hung up and wished to hell the butterflies in his stomach would settle down. He spent a few minutes making a list of the things he needed to do, like making sure to get a new tuxedo shirt and having the car detailed so it was perfect inside. He wondered if he should have flowers or something but decided that was too girly. Thankfully his thoughts turned back to work, and he was able to keep busy through the rest of the morning and into the afternoon when he had to go to the partners' meeting.

Gary sat at his place at the head of the table, and Malcolm took the spot at the other end. Carolyn Spencer, their divorce specialist, came in wearing her usual determined look. Corporate attorney Howard Brosig and criminal defense attorney Lyndon Mayer followed right behind.

"I think advertising is a good idea," Carolyn said right away.

"Of course you do. You handle divorce," Howard shot back. "But that kind of advertising does not look good for our corporate clients. They want discretion, and they bring in more money to the firm than divorces. If we do this, a lot of our current large clients will bail. They do not want to be associated with a television law firm."

"We need to bring in new clients," Gary said, defending his idea.

"This is not the way to do it," Lyndon insisted. "My clients want discretion. They do not pick their lawyer from a television ad. They're buying our reputation and stature when they come to us. If they wanted that type of lawyer, they'd call one of those 888 numbers. There are better ways of getting new clients. We have a table at the benefit this weekend. We're all going, and it's our job to talk to as many people in the room as possible. They are our potential clients."

"I still say that advertising the right way can be beneficial," Carolyn said.

"How would we do that?" Lyndon asked. "As far as I've seen, there isn't a way. Clients need to be cultivated through contacts, satisfaction, and word of mouth. I'm not opposed to marketing ourselves, just not with a television commercial… or radio, for that matter. Firms like that have their place, and some of them are very successful, almost enough to make me jealous, but that isn't the kind of firm I want to be associated with," he added firmly to Gary. "And quite frankly, I don't have to be."

"Lyndon, there isn't any need for that," Malcolm said calmly. "This is an idea that needs to be discussed, and Gary was right to bring it up. I do happen to think that this isn't for us, and if it comes up for a vote, it seems it will fail. But I also agree that we need to make a larger effort in marketing. There are other charity events that we can attend, and the money we would have spent on a commercial could be invested in professional marketing if that's the way we want to go." He looked at the other four people around the table. "Carolyn, would your clients be happy if part of your staff decamped?" He knew that was a possibility. They took as much pride in the firm as anyone.

"True," she said softly. "My staff is damned good, and I don't want to lose them."

It looked as though Gary's idea wasn't going to fly. "New clients are what we all need," Gary pressed.

"Let's get down to it. We've always built relationships with our clients. Some of them we've had for years. Turning our office into a production line isn't who we are, and that's what this will do. We all have contacts, and we need to use them." Malcolm looked right at Gary. That was the reason he'd been elected as senior partner.

"That's the old way of doing things," Gary countered.

"But it's the way we want to move forward," Lyndon said and stood up. "I have an appointment, and I won't go along with this." He turned and left the conference room. It looked to Malcolm as though the meeting was over. Gary seemed shell-shocked, and he left next, with Carolyn behind him.

"We have to do something," Howard said. "He isn't going to cut it, and I think we all see that now."

"But he was only elected three months ago."

Howard leaned forward. "The only reason he was elected to anything is because you weren't interested in running. You're more than qualified for the job, and you understand how to lead a firm. He's more interested in petty rules and control than he is in leading, and we need a leader." Howard stood. "I didn't want to think this, but the only reason he's here is because his father was here. Otherwise he'd never have made the grade, and now he's the one who's supposed to lead the ship. If he stays, there's an iceberg ahead with our name on it." Howard left the conference room, and Malcolm left as well and went to his office.

"You could have backed me," Gary said a few minutes later when he hurried inside and closed the door.

"I told you it wasn't a good idea. You need to lead, and that means bringing people along to your way of thinking as well as soliciting their ideas. Get consensus. That's what Harlan always did and what made him so good."

"I'm not Harlan," Gary said.

"No, you're not, and while you should put your spin on the job, you also need to have the skills he had." Malcolm sat down. "I have to get back to work, and I'm sure you have clients that require your attention." He knew he was dismissing Gary, but he couldn't do his job and Gary's as well. Gary wasn't happy, but he left his office and Malcolm got back to work.

THE REST of his week didn't go much better. He kept seeing impromptu meetings between the other partners, and at one time or another, each of them spoke to him about Gary. It seemed most of the firm's partners were losing faith in Gary quickly, and they were looking to him for leadership. Malcolm didn't want to do anything that would jeopardize the firm, and he still wasn't interested in serving as the senior partner. But the handwriting was quickly becoming visible on the wall, and he was going to have to make a decision.

For now Malcolm pushed that aside. It was Friday and he was headed home, a little nervous and excited. When he got home, he jumped into the shower and then dressed in his tuxedo, trying to decide on the tie he wanted to wear. When he and David had gone on their cruises, they'd dressed up, so he had a number of bow ties in various colors, but for tonight he decided on basic black because it always worked. Once he was dressed, he put on his black overcoat and left the house, following his GPS to Hans's address in Shorewood.

When Malcolm arrived, he parked and checked himself in the mirror, then took a deep breath to steady his nerves. He got out of the car, approached the house, and rang the bell.

The door opened, and Hans stood in the doorway, looking stunning in his tuxedo with a deep azure tie and cummerbund that set off his eyes in an amazing way.

"Wow," Malcolm mumbled. "You look great."

"Come on in. I need to get my coat and we can go." Malcolm stepped inside. "Do you need anything?" Hans asked as he got his things together.

"I'm good, thanks." Malcolm took the chance to look at Hans's house. The furniture was modern—clean, with a Scandinavian feel. In a way it was what Malcolm might have expected, but the overall effect with the use of color was warm and inviting. Solid furnishings that weren't fussy.

"I'm ready when you are," Hans said.

"Your home looks very comfortable."

"It is. I need warmth and comfort in order to work. Most of the time I sit in that chair right there and work for hours. It cradles me, and I can sit there and get lost in my stories." Hans smiled warmly and then turned away. "Ready?"

They left the house, and Malcolm opened the passenger door for Hans before heading around to his side and sliding into the seat. "How was your week?" he asked as he started the engine.

"Interesting. I was approached to write another adventure, and my agent was approached to see if I was interested in doing a series of science-fiction stories. I've always wanted to write them, but up until now I haven't had the chance. When you're starting out, making a bunch of unexpected changes can throw off readers, but my fan base is established enough that I can try some new things. How about you?"

"I'm getting a lot of pressure to step into the role of senior partner."

"That's great. Isn't that a good move for you?"

"It is, but it isn't something I think I want to do." The last time, he'd been able to use David's passing as an excuse to step aside, but this time, with the pressure the others were putting on him, he didn't have an easy way out. As much as Malcolm was propping Gary up, it didn't seem like it was going to work. "It's a lot of responsibility, and it's…."

"Well, whatever you decide to do, I'm sure you'll be amazing at it."

"I don't know." Malcolm had tried giving the idea some thought, but all he came back to was the pressure and responsibility and not being sure it was what he wanted.

"That doesn't seem like you. At least not the work you. When I was in your office, you were knowledgeable, confident, and seemed like you owned the place. If your peers think you can do it, why don't you?"

"Before David died I wanted to be senior partner, but afterward…." Malcolm took the on-ramp to the freeway and headed downtown. "I spent a lot of my life working. David and I had made a life, and then he was diagnosed and everything changed overnight. Instead of work and cases, it was chemotherapy and appointments. David became so much more important than anything in the office. I thought we had time, but it turned out we didn't. After he died and when I had nothing but time on my hands, I wasn't sure what I wanted, so I stepped aside when the previous senior partner retired, and I got behind Gary."

"How is that working out?"

"Not so well." Malcolm figured the internal politics of the office wasn't something Hans would be too interested in, so he tried to think of a way to change the subject. "I have to make a decision, and pretty soon. It's going to devastate Gary, but I have to think he can see it coming. Is your current manuscript coming along?"

"Yeah. It's really moving forward. The president is in peril, and I'm just about to put the entire world order in jeopardy." Hans wrung his hands. "I love it when I can do that."

He sounded like a supervillain, and Malcolm chuckled.

"I get to blow things up, flatten Beijing, and even have a new continent rise out of the Pacific, sending catastrophic waves in every direction, and when I'm done, I go to bed and sleep like a baby."

"You really do like your job."

"I do."

Hans turned toward him, flashing a million-watt smile, and Malcolm almost missed the turn off the freeway. He managed to get over and took the spur downtown and got off at the exit closest to the art museum. Malcolm parked in the structure across the street and escorted Hans out and up to the plaza level. They crossed the bridge that led to the museum entrance. It was cold, and snow covered the museum landscaping, but the wind was low, and the stars filled the sky.

"Have you been here before?" Malcolm asked when he saw Hans taking in everything.

"No. I knew about it, and I've seen the building as I've driven by, but I haven't been in. The place is stunning, and the way they have it and the sail lit is amazing."

The building was reminiscent of a ship in form, with a solar shade that opened and closed. When it was open, it made the building look like it was under sail. The effect was stunning under the lights.

He couldn't have agreed more. He stayed close to Hans as they crossed the rest of the way and stepped down the stairs to enter the museum lobby. The open space glittered with crystal centerpieces and light that seemed to come from everywhere. The actual museum was closed, but that didn't matter. The evening held an excitement that Malcolm couldn't help feeling. Malcolm took their coats to the check and then returned to where Hans waited and escorted him over to the table the firm had arranged.

"Carolyn, Howard, Gary, Lyndon, this is my guest for the evening, Hans." He greeted each person and waited while Carolyn introduced her husband—number three if Malcolm wasn't mistaken. It amazed Malcolm that three men had been willing to risk a marriage to ball-busting Carolyn, but she and Brent seemed happy enough.

"This is my date, Jennifer," Gary said as they went around the table.

Malcolm and Hans greeted both of them before saying hello to Lyndon's wife, Maxine, and Howard's girlfriend, Wendy. They took their seats and chatted a few minutes. Howard excused himself to get something from the bar, and Malcolm did the same, quietly asking Hans what he'd like.

"A martini would be perfect," Hans said with a smile.

Malcolm followed Howard as he threaded through the tables. "Didn't I see your date at the office?" Howard asked. "You aren't dating a client, are you? Gary will have a conniption if you are." He looked back at Gary, and Malcolm got the feeling Howard would sell tickets if that happened.

"Hans *was* a client. Our business was concluded, and we met again while my brother was here. He seemed nice, and we had a lot to talk about." Malcolm shifted to see how long the line was. They were going to be a while, and Howard didn't seem convinced. "I was out to dinner with my brother, and Hans had been stood up by a blind date. Peter asked him to join us, and he and I hit it off. Hans gave his phone number to my brother." He smiled at how ridiculous it sounded.

"Very tenth grade," Howard teased.

"Exactly. Peter said he'd never stop pestering me until I asked Hans out, and since this was a public place, I thought it would be a good idea." Besides, it seemed Hans had captured the attention of half the room, especially the women.

"What does he do?"

"Hans Erickson, the author."

Howard stopped, his mouth hanging open. "That's him?" Howard had given Malcolm the first of Hans's books for his birthday a few years earlier. "You aren't bullshitting me."

"Of course not. That's really him. He lives in Shorewood now."

From the way Howard was grinning, Malcolm expected him to go full-on rock-star-worthy fanboy any second. "Do you think he'd sign something for me? I could put it in one of my books. That would be so awesome."

"You can ask him," Malcolm said. He turned toward where Hans was sitting at the table talking to the others. They all seemed enthralled, and when Malcolm and Howard finally got to the front of the line, they got their drinks and made their way back to the table.

"Hans is the author of those books you like," Wendy said to Howard. "He's been entertaining us with stories of some of his adventures. He went on a hunting safari in Africa." She looked hopefully at Howard, who sighed.

"We need to get you a passport first," he told her softly.

"I know. But that sounds so cool. And he's a diver. You could take me diving somewhere. We could learn together."

Wendy leaned close, and Malcolm wasn't sure what she whispered to Howard, but he turned beet red and nodded once. Obviously she had given him some incentive.

The servers fanned out through the room, placing salads at each plate. "This looks nice," Hans said. The salad wasn't anything particularly special, but Malcolm was happy Hans was willing to make the most of the evening.

"I'm glad you're enjoying yourself," Malcolm told Hans and felt Hans squeeze his hand under the table.

"I really am. Your colleagues are quite nice," he said as he looked across the table. "What's with the girl with Gary?" he whispered without moving his lips.

Malcolm shrugged and kept the smile on his face.

"How did you meet?" Carolyn asked.

"I met Malcolm the first time at the office. I was there on business, and it would have stayed that way if we hadn't met again last weekend. He and his brother took pity on me after a blind date stood me up, and Malcolm and I hit it off."

Dang, there was that smile again, and the dancing blue eyes.

"Malcolm and I have quite a bit in common, and I think we understand some important things about each other."

Hans took a bite of his salad, and Malcolm let go of some of his nerves. Gary and the others didn't seem fazed by Hans at all. They'd all liked David, so having someone new in his life might have caused problems. Once the dishes were being cleared and before the next course was served, Lyndon and his wife excused themselves and wound between the tables to one a few over, where they talked to the CFO of a local microbrewery. The business was small but growing.

"Is there someone you need to talk to?" Hans asked.

Malcolm nodded with a smile. "Come with me. You'll make his day." Malcolm stood and took Hans's hand without really thinking about it. They made their way to one of the very front tables.

"Mal," Claudette Gilbert said as she stood. "How are you?" They exchanged cheek kisses.

"I'm wonderful."

Her gaze shifted to Hans, revealing joy mixed with curiosity.

"This is Hans Erickson," Malcolm said. "He's here with me this evening, and I thought that he and Zephyr might have something in common."

Claudette's grandson stood from the seat next to his grandmother. "You're *the* Hans Erickson? I have one of your books with me." He beamed and pulled a book out of his backpack. "Would you sign it?"

Claudette had been one of the first clients to take a chance on Malcolm, and they had been friends ever since. Malcolm had met Zephyr many times, and he'd never seen the fifteen-year-old without a book.

"Certainly," Hans said and stepped away to sign the book.

"How is Zephyr doing?" Malcolm asked Claudette.

"He's in remission, and we're hoping it stays that way." She followed Zephyr with her gaze. His hair was growing back, and he'd lost some of the haunted expression he'd had during treatment. It even looked like he'd started putting on weight.

"We all do."

"How are you?" Claudette looked at Hans. "Are you dating?"

"Hans and I are exploring a friendship." God, he hoped that was what was happening. "It's too early for me to take things too seriously, but Hans is…." He wasn't sure how to put it, but the smile on Zephyr's face said it all as he and Hans talked.

"Honey, I know that look."

"He's a new friend. I'm not a kid any longer."

"Hon, neither of us is. But that doesn't need to stop us. I know you're still hurting. It took me a long time to get over Larry's passing. And I still love him. He's been gone eight years, and there isn't a day that I don't still miss him. But I've been out with other men, and I even fell in love once."

"But it didn't work out?"

"There were extenuating circumstances."

Malcolm guessed that was her way of saying that his intentions weren't entirely honorable—in other words, he was after her money.

"That hurt too, but not as much as losing Larry. The thing is, it's okay to fall in love again. I did it with the wrong man, but I still had fun." She bumped his arm. "Let yourself be happy." She turned away. "Zephyr, sweetheart, let Mr. Erickson go. We need to return to our places. They're serving the next course."

They went back to their chairs, and Malcolm and Hans made their way back to theirs.

"Thank you. That meant a lot to him."

"How come he just happened to have a copy of my book?" Hans asked as they reached the table.

"Well, he reads all the time, but I may have told his grandmother that Zephyr would have need of it," Malcolm answered. "He's been through a lot, and after he was diagnosed, his grandmother threw herself into his care. This was her idea, and as you can see, the room is full of people who paid two hundred dollars a plate for the evening. Besides, have you ever made anyone so happy?"

"I don't think so," Hans answered. "He asked me all about each of the characters and if they were going to be in any more stories. It's like they're real to him."

"Maybe when you've been through what he has, imagination becomes even more important. And you helped provide that."

"Are you a friend of the family?"

"Of a sort. She's been a client for years, but it was Zephyr and David who brought us closer. The two of them met during treatments. They were both on the same basic schedule, so they saw each other at the hospital, and leave it to David to strike up a friendship anywhere." Malcolm was vaguely aware of the others around the table listening to him as servers set the plates. "Of course, I knew Claudette already, but over time we grew closer. Zephyr is her daughter's only child, and Claudette has raised him since he was four after her daughter died. Claudette is quite a woman."

He turned away and began to eat. He needed something to do as the grief got too close to the surface. Talking about loss always brought his own to the front, and he didn't want to break down in front of his colleagues.

"It's all right," Hans whispered. "You aren't alone." Hans lightly squeezed his arm out of sight of the others, and Malcolm felt better.

Malcolm nodded and slowly looked up from his roast beef, hoping like hell the others hadn't noticed. The fact that every set of eyes around the table was looking at him told Malcolm more than he needed to know.

"So once, when I was off the coast of South America, I was with a team diving on a wreck," Hans said. "We were getting so close to our goal. We'd found some evidence that this particular ship had been carrying Spanish gold. We'd been diving on her for about three days and coming up with nothing, when this school of fish starts rolling and swooping all around us. They were stunning, and it was so cool."

Malcolm wiped his eyes with his napkin, listening to Hans as the others were.

"Then the school scatters in all directions, and sure enough, a huge shark glides right nearby. This thing was massive, a Great White, and let me tell you, those teeth were something else. This guy was having a fish feast, and then he spied me. I was a sitting duck."

"What did you do?" Carolyn asked breathlessly.

"I wasn't too deep, so I sent up a screen of bubbles to try to hide and swam toward the boat. When I broke the surface, I was twenty feet or so from the boat. To this day I don't know how I got back into it. The other men all swore that I'm living proof that you can walk on water."

Everyone laughed, including Malcolm, and then they returned to their meals. Malcolm looked at Hans, thanking him with his eyes before eating once again. Hans responded with another light squeeze on his arm.

Light table conversation lasted through the rest of the meal, and then people began to mingle and work the room a little, talking and laughing. Malcolm made sure to say hello to the people he knew, received a few inquiries, and was promised that he'd be receiving some phone calls because his advice and expertise were required. That was the main purpose of these events for him, to be seen and meet people, in addition to helping the charity.

Half an hour after dinner, some of the tables were cleared away and a band began to play. Couples started making their way to the dance floor.

"Would anyone like a drink?" Howard asked before heading off toward the bar.

"I'll be right back," Hans said and pushed his chair back.

Malcolm watched him go and then glanced around the room, watching people. He saw that Claudette had dragged Zephyr onto the dance floor. They seemed to be having a decent time. Malcolm felt himself falling into another funk until he sensed someone standing beside him. He turned, and Hans extended a hand.

"You want to dance?" Malcolm asked. Hans nodded once and held his hand steady. Malcolm stood and took it, letting Hans lead him to the floor. Once they reached it, Malcolm pulled Hans into position and led him around the floor.

David had loved dancing, and it was an activity the two of them had enjoyed. Hans was terrific, and together they were respectable. "Thank you for earlier," Malcolm said as he looked into Hans's eyes.

"It was nothing." Hans said as he pulled him a little closer. "You needed a few minutes, and I could give you that."

"I had no idea things would still be so hard after all these months."

"Everyone grieves at their own pace. You lost someone closest to your heart. You need to feel the pain, process it, and then let it go. It's the last part that's the hardest," Hans continued, following him around the floor. "You know people are looking at us."

"Not us, you. Mostly they're wondering what a hot, handsome guy like you is doing dancing with an old wreck like me."

Hans scoffed. "I think it's the silver fox that's getting all the attention."

"Me?"

"Yeah. You're the one who looks completely edible in that tuxedo."

Malcolm listened for any sort of signal that Hans was kidding and heard none.

"Come on." He was finding that hard to believe. "My man-hunting days are long over."

"I don't think so," Hans said, and he surprised Malcolm by running his fingers lightly over his cheek. "You have to realize that you're an attractive man."

"I'm way too old to be attractive," Malcolm protested.

Hans rolled his eyes. "You don't know what you are." He stroked his face once again. "That's what you need to find out. For many years you were Malcolm, David's husband. Now you're just Malcolm, and that's hard to get used to. But you will."

Malcolm wasn't sure if Hans was right or not, but at the moment he was less concerned with things like that than he was with the warmth that spread from inside. It was like he'd been asleep for a long time and now he was starting to wake up. The song ended and another began, this one slower and quieter. Malcolm stopped, but Hans didn't release him.

"Now it's my turn to lead." Hans tugged him closer until they were chest to chest, and Malcolm could feel Hans's breath kissing his neck.

"Hans…," Malcolm said, feeling a little panicky.

"It's just a dance, and I'm willing to bet it's been a long time since someone held you and was there just for you. I know what it was like to care for someone who's ill, to have every ounce of your energy directed at him and his care. Just let go for a few minutes and let someone else care for you."

Malcolm sighed and closed his eyes. He could do that, and it felt good to be held and touched again. He'd done plenty of holding when David was sick, but having someone understand that he needed to be held was so comforting. "Hans, I…."

"It's all right. This is just a dance."

"I was going to say that this…."

The word escaped him, but Hans simply tightened his hold a little bit, and Malcolm knew he understood. Malcolm closed his eyes and let the movement carry him to a happier place than he'd been in quite a while. He'd been living, but only just barely.

All too soon the song ended, and Hans let him go and stepped away. They walked back to the table and sat down. Most of the other seats were empty, with only Lyndon and his wife sitting together, talking softly.

"We were talking about Gary's date," Lyndon said quietly.

Malcolm had been wondering if things would be strained after dancing, but obviously not. "She added nothing to the conversation and seemed to want to be anywhere but here." It was unfortunate but true that Gary was so preoccupied with appearances that he'd need to have the best-looking date at the table.

"She was bored stiff and kept looking around the room."

"Where are they now?"

"Gary is talking to a man over there," Hans said, "and it looks like his date is much more interested in someone else."

Hans tilted his head to the other side. Gary's date—Malcolm couldn't remember her name—was sitting at another table, making eyes at and laughing with another man. They seemed deep in conversation, and she looked happy, or at least engaged.

"What's Gary doing?" Hans asked, and Malcolm turned to follow Hans's gaze.

Gary was talking animatedly to a man in his early twenties. They seemed to be discussing something intently, and the young man looked about ready to punch Gary. Malcolm got up and hurried over just as Gary punched the younger man, catching him on the shoulder, and the young man used the momentum and let loose with his other fist, inadvertently catching Malcolm on the arm. Malcolm went down, sprawling on the gleaming marble museum floor, and instantly Hans was there beside him. Gary beat a hasty retreat, and the slugger apologized profusely and backed away. It was all a little surreal and a lot painful. Malcolm was sure his arm wasn't broken, but pain shot up and down it for a few moments before it began to ease.

"Did you hurt anything besides your arm?" Hans asked, and Malcolm shook his head. "Can you get up?"

"Yes. I'll be fine." Malcolm got to his feet and slowly made his way back to the table and sat down. He cradled his arm, and Hans sat next to him. "I don't have a clue what that was all about."

"I can try to find out," Hans said, but Malcolm shook his head. It would all come out when he went back to the office, he was sure. Thankfully the music had started again, and everyone seemed to be letting what happened fall away in deference to the occasion.

"I'm sorry, sir," the man who'd hit him said just above the music. "You weren't supposed to get in the way."

He sat down nervously, and Hans rose and stepped in front of him.

"It's all right, Hans," Malcolm said, warmed by Hans's protective nature. "What was going on?"

"Gary…. He…." The man looked around. "He was here with my girlfriend. Now former girlfriend, I guess. What she sees in him, I have no idea, but…." He grabbed a napkin off the table and twisted it in his hands. "He's such a weasel."

At least that answered the earlier question. "Why wasn't your girlfriend here with you tonight? Didn't you ask her?"

"I'm here for a work thing, and they didn't have extra tickets…."

"Did it ever occur to you that the reason she came with Gary was to make you jealous? She obviously wanted to come, so…."

He shrugged. "Well, I came over to apologize again." He stood and walked away.

"You know, Mal," a friend said from behind him, "I know a good personal injury lawyer if you need one."

"Gee, thanks," Malcolm quipped back with a smile, glad he could laugh about it. His arm still hurt, but he knew it was best to try to put it behind them so the incident didn't cloud the evening.

It seemed Gary was nowhere to be found, and when Hans got Malcolm a glass of water and a double Scotch, Malcolm drank both and sat back.

"What are you thinking about?"

Malcolm groaned. "That like it or not, I just became the senior partner at Warren, Hanlan, and Webber. The partners are all going to want Gary's head on Monday, and I won't be able to stop it. We need a senior partner, and they all want me for the job." He stood up. "Is it okay if we leave?"

"Whatever you want to do," Hans said.

Malcolm handed Hans the coat check, and he went to get them.

"You all right?" a man asked.

Malcolm nodded.

"I've been meaning to come talk to you, but you always seemed occupied, and I didn't want to interrupt. I'm Taylor Donovan. My company is having a problem, and I believe I need your help."

Malcolm extended his good hand and then reached into his coat pocket. He pulled out a card. "Please call my office first thing on Monday, and I'll be happy to talk to you. I know I have some time." He smiled and met Taylor's intense gaze. This was a man on a mission, and a man who was worried about something. That was clear enough.

"Thank you," Taylor said with a half smile and then turned away, sliding the card into his pocket.

Hans returned, and Malcolm carefully put on his coat. Then, after saying good-bye to a few people, he and Hans left for the evening, making their way back out into the cold and across the bridge to the parking structure. "I should drive," Hans said as they reached the car. "You just had a double scotch, and I haven't had anything to drink in a while."

Malcolm handed over his keys and directed Hans back to his house. He didn't give much thought at that point to how Hans was going to get home. All he wanted was to get home himself, take something for the ache in his arm, and go to bed.

By the time they reached his house, the alcohol had kicked in fully. Malcolm was warm from the inside, and his head was a little swimmy. Maybe it was the drink or the endorphins from the pain. It could also be the gentle touch Hans had as he helped him inside and got him settled in a chair.

"I'm going to be fine."

"I know that. But you can't drive, and I don't want to take your car." Hans went into the kitchen, returned with a couple of glasses of water, and handed one to him. Then he sat on the sofa near him. "You're an interesting man, Malcolm."

"Why? I always thought I was boring." He sipped some water and set the glass on a coaster on the side table.

"Then you're wrong. You have a heart, and when it comes down to it, a spine of steel. You're willing to try to help someone attain his dream, even if he isn't able to keep it."

"Gary?" Malcolm asked.

"He wanted to be senior partner, and you helped get him elected and gave him a chance. It isn't your fault that he didn't make the most of it. He should have valued the gift you gave him."

"What gift?" Malcolm wasn't sure what he meant.

"The chance. At some point in our lives, someone gives us a chance. Success is what we make of it. My first editor, Nicole, bought my first book, not because it was the greatest story ever written, but because she saw something in me. She published *Undersea Inferno* and then the next one, each getting better and better, selling more and more. She believed in me, and I made the most of her faith. You did the same thing for Gary, but he didn't follow through, and that isn't your fault. It's his, and he's the one who needs to own up to it when the time comes."

Malcolm wasn't sure Gary was capable of that. In fact, the more he thought about it, the more he realized that this whole thing was his fault for getting Gary's hopes up. After all, he was the one who helped create this monster, and now he was going to have to deal with the fallout. Gary was certain to be removed by the other partners, and he could end up leaving the firm. Maybe that was for the best for all of them.

"Do you want me to take you home in a few hours?" Malcolm asked.

"That's fine," Hans said, and Malcolm got up and made his way to the kitchen. He took some painkillers he had in the cupboard. Then he found some snacks and brought them into the living room. When he returned, he took off his jacket and removed his tie before loosening his shirt. It felt good to be more comfortable. Hans did the same, and Malcolm found a movie to rent and sat on the sofa to be closer to the food.

"Thank God it's the weekend."

"I know exactly how you feel," Hans said, and they both put their feet up as the movie started.

MALCOLM WASN'T sure how much he actually watched, but he did wake up for the dramatic climax when Bruce Willis was about to take out the bad guy. Hans had fallen asleep as well and was leaning against him. Part of Malcolm told him he should move away, and the other half urged him to stay right where he was. Malcolm liked being close to someone, and Hans was nice. But he didn't want to give him the wrong idea. Eventually Hans woke and straightened up slowly.

"Sorry."

"Don't be," Malcolm said.

"Okay, I won't." Hans smiled and turned, leaning a little closer. "I know you aren't ready, and I'm not going to push you, but I really like you, Malcolm." He slowly moved his head closer. "You're a wonderful guy, and I've been looking for someone like you for a very long time. I don't have much luck with men, as my last relationship will attest, but I think my luck can change with you."

"Hans, I…. It's only been a year, and…."

"I know. So I'd really like to be friends."

Malcolm could feel the energy coursing between them, and his better judgment told him that wasn't the best idea. Not that he didn't want to be friends with Hans, but he wasn't sure it was possible to remain just friends. Already Malcolm was warm, and his heart beat a little faster just because Hans looked at him as though he was starving and Malcolm was a buffet lunch. Part of him wanted to give in and say to hell with it, but he knew it would end badly, and that wasn't fair to him or to Hans. "I…." It was on the tip of his tongue to say no, but he ended up nodding.

"Excellent," Hans said and then did the last thing Malcolm expected: he kissed him. Not hard, but it was enough to send Malcolm's lips tingling.

"You usually kiss your friends?"

"Sorry." Hans moved back. "I shouldn't have done that. It was too much, and I did promise we could be friends." Hans got to his feet. He put on his jacket and placed his tie in his pocket. Then he got his coat. "I don't want to be a problem, but it's probably best if you take me home."

Malcolm thought that was best as well. He gathered the dishes and took them to the kitchen before getting his coat. As soon as they stepped out of the house, the cold assaulted Malcolm. Any residual effects of the Scotch were instantly gone. He locked the door and hurried down the walk to the car. Once they were buckled in, he started the car and pulled out.

Neither of them talked very much along the way. It wasn't a particularly long drive from Whitefish Bay to Shorewood. Malcolm knew he should say something, but he wasn't sure what. Hans had surprised him with the kiss. But it was only a kiss, and he was an adult. He certainly should have been able to deal with it.

Too soon Malcolm pulled into Hans's driveway. He definitely should say something. The silence had gone way past comfortable. Malcolm pulled to a stop and turned to Hans, who opened his door, the cold air surging inside.

"I had a nice time this evening. I hope your arm is okay." Hans got out of the car. "I'll see you later." He closed the door, and Malcolm watched as Hans hurried inside. The lights came on in the living room, and Malcolm pulled out of the drive and began the journey home.

When he got there, Malcolm went right upstairs and undressed, hung up his tuxedo, and then went through his nightly routine before climbing into bed. He knew he'd overreacted, but he wasn't ready to be kissing anyone other than David.

His phone vibrated, and Malcolm checked it, answering the call when he saw it was Peter.

"So how did it go?" Peter asked.

"You really are worse than Mom ever was."

"Don't give me that. How did it go? Is he still there? I don't want details, but did you have a good evening or a world-shattering evening?"

"Good Lord," Malcolm groaned.

"That bad?"

"It was a nice evening, and I got back a little while ago from dropping Hans off at his house."

"Okay, what happened?" Peter asked. "Come on. You wouldn't be pissy if it had gone perfectly, so what happened? Did he burp or say something stupid?"

"No."

"Then what?"

"He kissed me."

Silence on the other side of the line. "Okay. That's bad?"

"I'm not ready. I knew this was a bad idea." Malcolm wanted to hang up and go to bed.

"It was a great idea, and he kissed you. That's good."

"No, it wasn't," Malcolm protested.

"Why?" Peter asked immediately, and the line grew quiet. Malcolm knew Peter was waiting for an answer. "I can wait here all night if I have to."

"Because I liked it," Malcolm whispered and clamped his eyes closed. "I liked that he kissed me. It's been a long time, and maybe I'm just lonely, but I miss David, and I'm tired of spending all my time sitting in this house looking at what's left of the life we had together." Malcolm got up and began to pace the room, ignoring the chill.

"What did you do?" Peter asked.

"I freaked out like some vestal virgin and took him home. Now I think I messed things up permanently."

"If you aren't ready for that sort of thing, then maybe that's for the best. I'm sorry I pushed you so hard. Maybe you were right and I should have left you alone."

Malcolm knew that act. He'd been to that little play more times than he could count, and he wasn't going to bite. "Don't be passive-aggressive. You don't do it as well as you used to."

"Fine. It was only a kiss, and one that you said you liked." Peter paused for a second. "Are you sure this isn't just guilt? You kissed Hans, and now you're feeling guilty out of some misplaced sense that you're somehow cheating on David? Because if you are, I'm going to fly back to town and smack you on the side of the head. I liked David. He was a great brother-in-law. Hell, there were times when I liked him more than I liked you. But I know he'd be angry as hell if you hung on like that. David was fun, and he'd want you to go on living… and you did, for once."

"Okay, okay," Malcolm said. "What do I do now?"

"How should I know? If you want, I can put Susan on. She's great with stuff like that."

"No. I'll figure it out myself. Thanks for listening."

"No problem, Mal. Now go to bed and get some rest." They said good night, and Malcolm ended the call, suddenly feeling every chill in the room. He climbed under the covers and pulled them up around his neck, rolling onto his side, willing the sheets to warm.

He wasn't any closer to answers an hour later, but he did feel better and had resolved to talk to Hans, if he'd take his calls. Maybe they could be friends. He needed some of those, and Hans had already seen him at his hot-and-cold worst. The only flaw in that plan seemed to be the fact that his lips still tingled when he thought about that kiss.

Chapter 4

"MORNING, MALCOLM," Jane said when he arrived at the office. She had his calendar and coffee ready, just as she usually did. "How was the dinner?"

"It was nice. You should have gone." He had offered to get her a pair of tickets. Malcolm gingerly set down his case. He was still babying his bruised arm a little.

"Why are you holding your arm that way?" she asked as Malcolm sat down.

"I got punched protecting Gary from an enraged boyfriend." He settled in his chair and got comfortable.

"Is that why you look like crap?" She stepped forward and began fussing with his tie.

"Okay, I'll give you the condensed version. I had fun. Hans and I danced. It was nice. I stepped in to break up a fight between Gary and his date's boyfriend and took the punch. My shoulder is bruised, and it hurts. We left after that. At my house Hans kissed me, but I freaked, so I doubt he's going to want to see me anymore. I feel like an idiot, and now I'm going to have to deal with the fallout of Gary's bad behavior." Malcolm glared at Jane. "And so help me, if any of this makes it to the office gossip mill through you, I will personally see that you get reassigned as Gary's assistant."

"Jesus. It was that bad?"

Malcolm groaned as he slowly began to type.

"What can I do to help?"

"Nothing, unless you have a way to make me feel less stupid for freaking out about a kiss." He didn't look up from his screen. "I don't know why I'm talking to you about this."

"Because you need someone to listen, and shame on you, Malcolm. I never spread rumors—you know that."

She stormed out of the office, and Malcolm sighed. He felt like total crap, so he figured he might as well spread the fucking love. He got to work in peace for fifteen minutes until Jane whirlwinded back in.

"Okay. Your first appointment is in ten minutes, and here...." She plopped a small catalog on the desk and opened it. "I suggest these. They're nice for an apology and don't look too girly."

"Flowers?" Malcolm looked at the catalog and then up at her.

Jane rolled her eyes. "Yes. You like him, don't you?" She continued without waiting for his answer. "If you do, then...." She stabbed the catalog. "When a man has been an ass, he shall send flowers. It's like the twelfth commandment. The eleventh is 'don't be an ass.'" She set the file on his desk as well and once again left the office.

Malcolm shook his head and picked up the phone. He ended up sending two arrangements, one to Hans and the other to Jane. He desperately needed her on his side, and he hated when she was angry with him.

His first appointment arrived, and he started his day, grateful that the office was quiet. In fact, it was the kind of quiet that couldn't last, like the few seconds of silence before a bomb goes off, but thankfully it lasted until an hour before he was set to leave.

MALCOLM GOT home very late that night, dragging himself into the house. Once inside, he sat on the sofa and nearly fell asleep right there. Only his phone vibrating insistently kept him from falling asleep. "Hello."

"Malcolm? You sound tired. I'm sorry if I woke you."

"It's all right, Hans. I just got home from the office. It was one hell of a day."

"The fallout from the party?" Hans asked.

"Yeah, and it was worse than I could ever have imagined." Malcolm breathed deeply, trying to take in all that had happened. "I don't know how I'm going to be able to handle all this." He began to shake a little.

"I called because I got the flowers you sent. That was very thoughtful of you."

Malcolm was too tired and turned around to really think very clearly at the moment. He kept inhaling deeply, but he couldn't get enough oxygen, so he inhaled again and again. "Sorry," he gasped. "I'm having…."

"You're hyperventilating. Grab a paper bag and breathe into it," Hans said.

"I need to go," Malcolm gasped and hung up. He continued breathing erratically and stood up, trying to get to the kitchen. His thinking was muddled, but he managed to get to the closet and grab a paper bag. He crumpled the opening and put it over his mouth.

The crinkling filled his ears as the bag contracted and inflated. After a few minutes he began feeling better and went back into the living room. He sat down and tried to clear his mind. Worrying and fretting wouldn't change anything.

Malcolm jumped at the doorbell and got up, still carrying the bag in case the panic returned. He opened the door, and Hans raced inside.

"Are you all right?" Hans asked.

"Yes," Malcolm answered. "What are you doing here?"

Hans looked at him like he was from outer space. "You had some sort of attack while we were on the phone, and you expect me to stay home and wonder if you're okay? I'm only two miles away, and I was lucky there were no cops." Hans took off his coat and took Malcolm's arm. "Go on in and sit down. I'll make some tea."

"Tea?" He wanted something stronger, but he figured Hans would fight him on it. Malcolm wasn't even sure if he had any tea in the cupboards. He never drank it. David had been a huge tea aficionado and kept an entire cupboard with all his blends. Malcolm had given it away a few months ago. Clearing out that cupboard had been more difficult than packing up David's clothes. "I can make coffee," Malcolm offered.

"I found what I was looking for," Hans called back, and Malcolm settled in his seat.

If Hans wanted to try to help, he wasn't going to fight it. It seemed he'd been fighting too many battles, and it was catching up with him. Malcolm waited, and Hans came in with two mugs and handed him one before sitting next to him on the sofa.

Malcolm tried very hard not to follow the denim that encased Hans's legs up his thighs and then…. He swallowed and took a sip of the tea and nearly choked, coughing as he set the mug on the table. "I guess drinking anything isn't a good idea right now."

"Do you want to tell me what happened?" Hans asked. "Was it what you thought?"

"It was that and worse. We called a partners' meeting, and two of the other partners asked Gary to step down. He refused because his self-identity is totally wrapped up in his job. So then they informed him that enough of the partners agreed that they have lost confidence in his leadership, and that they were prepared to force him to step down. This time Carolyn stepped in, and in the end she sided with them."

"What about you?" Hans asked.

"I stayed out of it. They didn't need me to add gasoline to the fire. Finally Gary agreed to step down, and then he resigned from the firm. Not that we're going to lose a great deal, because his client base is the smallest of any of us. The office is going to be in a tailspin for days after this, though." Malcolm sighed. "Then the other three turned to me, expecting I'd step up and take the job."

"Did you?"

"For the good of the firm, I did. So now I'm the managing partner. I have a full client load, and everyone in the entire office is going to come to me with their problems. I don't know how I can do all this and remain sane. Gary asked his assistant to go with him, but Ellen declined. I guess that told us a lot about how he was to work for, but I don't have a position for her. And tomorrow I have the honor of explaining all of this to the staff so that we can get back to business as quickly as possible."

"All right. I know you're overwhelmed, but you already know what you need to do."

"Enlighten me. My brain is completely dead at the moment."

"Well, as for Ellen, have her work for you. Let her manage the senior-partner portion of your job, and have Jane continue to manage your caseload like she does now. If you're going to do both jobs, then have the right help to do them. As for addressing the office, pretend it's court and give one hell of a summation. And you have room for a new partner, so decide who you want that to be. Advancement within the firm is always positive, isn't it?"

"I suppose." He hadn't really had a chance to think about it. David was always the one he could talk things over with, and when all this had happened, he'd missed him something terrible. His first instinct, even after all this time, had been to reach for the phone. The bad thing was that he still had David's number programmed into it, and he had nearly dialed it.

"You can do this. I know you have good role models you can draw on, and after what you said Gary did, you know what not to do."

"I know." The honest answer was that before David had gotten sick, Malcolm would have jumped at this chance. It would be a challenge, and at that time he would have reveled in the opportunities. Now, he…. God, he didn't know what he was or who he'd turned into. "I hate running away."

"And that's what you feel you're doing?" Hans asked.

"I don't know. I used to want this, and now…. All I want is to have my life quiet and settled. I've been told I'm acting like a turtle and that it's time to come out of my shell." Malcolm picked up his mug and sipped some tea. This time it went down smoothly and warmed him from the inside.

"Maybe it is. But that's for you to decide, not anyone else. I know your partners have forced you out of your shell a little by pushing this senior partner position on you, but do you honestly think you can't do this job well?"

"I know I can," Malcolm said.

"Then don't worry about it and enjoy it. This is a challenge for you, and maybe that's what you need right now, something different to occupy your mind and give you a new direction."

Malcolm knew Hans was right. He did need something to snap him out of the rut he'd been in for months. He'd just been getting by, doing his job and trying to keep the ache and pain of loss at bay.

"And for what it's worth, I know I pushed you too quickly and got carried away before. I really do appreciate the flowers and the sentiment behind them, but what happened wasn't your fault—it was mine."

Hans was definitely sincere, but the way he looked at Malcolm sent heat racing through him. Malcolm wished like hell he could figure out what it was. He kept thinking it was Hans's eyes. They always reminded him of David. But that wasn't it. There was something more pulling him to Hans.

"No, it wasn't. You kissed me, and it was a nice kiss." Damn, he could feel his cheeks heating up, and as much as he wanted to turn away from Hans, he couldn't.

"I think it was a little more than nice." Hans grinned slyly, and Malcolm knew Hans had seen his reaction. "In fact, I can tell you're thinking about it right now."

"I thought you were going to give me some time," Malcolm said and then swallowed hard. Hans hadn't moved, but Malcolm sure wished he would. He'd already told himself that if Hans kissed him again, he wouldn't balk or run. He wanted to be touched and held. Yes, Hans wasn't David, but he could accept that. Maybe it was time he began moving on. The notion chilled him but couldn't compete with the way Hans stoked fires Malcolm had thought were long dead.

"Is that what you really want? I can give you time and distance. But in my books, and I think this applies here as well, sometimes I like to shock my characters and give them the one thing they think they don't need, but deep down they know it's the one thing they want more than anything."

"I don't understand a thing you just said." Malcolm smiled nervously, afraid to look away. Whatever was happening between them had his palms sweating and his heart racing. His breathing grew more rapid, and he wondered if he needed the paper bag again, but the panic from earlier didn't rise again. Instead, in its place there was heat and a touch of fear.

"That's okay. You don't have to."

Hans slid closer on the sofa and lifted his hand slowly. It was like he was afraid any fast movement might spook Malcolm. When Hans made contact with the base of Malcolm's neck, he stiffened slightly and then eased into the caress. Hans cupped the back of his neck, strengthening his hold and then drawing Malcolm closer.

"I'm going to try this again. You've been sending me mixed signals. If you don't want me to continue, say something now."

Malcolm held his breath and said nothing. He wasn't sure he'd be able to tell him yes, but he certainly wasn't going to tell Hans no for a second time. His heart raced too fast, and his left foot bounced on the floor. Finally he nodded, and Hans closed the distance between them.

The kiss was soft at first but deepened quickly. Malcolm closed his eyes and floated on the touch for a few seconds before slamming back to earth with a body-shuddering jolt of lust and desire. The heat that had been simmering now bubbled over. Malcolm slowly encircled Hans with his arms. His aches and grief eased along with his worries, replaced by something much more basic.

Malcolm felt alive. When Hans pulled away for a second, he wondered what was wrong, but Hans surged back, nibbling at his upper lip and firmly caressing the back of his neck. Malcolm was being kissed, thoroughly, deeply, and even though Hans was only touching him in two places, he felt it from head to toe. Every nerve was on fire, and yet Malcolm held back for another few seconds before tightening his hold and bringing Hans even closer, melding their body heat to a near inferno. He hadn't felt anything like this for a long time, and damn if it didn't drive him nearly wild.

Hans pressed him back, and Malcolm offered no resistance. The sofa cushions molded to Malcolm's back as Hans settled on top of him. Malcolm kept his eyes closed, kissing him hard. His body thrummed with excitement he never thought he would feel again. Guilt niggled around the edges of his thoughts, but Malcolm pushed it away and concentrated on being desired once again.

"Malcolm, open your eyes," Hans whispered, and he opened his eyes, staring into Hans's. "I need you to see that this is me."

"I know who's with me." Malcolm guessed that Hans was afraid he was imagining David. But the way Hans touched him was so different. David had always been very gentle and caring. His touches had always been firm but on the softer side. Hans was different. He was demanding, strong, with an energy that Malcolm had never experienced before. It was erotic, and the banked power added to the intensity.

"Good," Hans said and tugged Malcolm's shirt out of his pants, sliding his hand up over Malcolm's belly. Damn, that felt mind-blowingly awesome, and Malcolm shivered. "Do you like being touched?"

Malcolm nodded and hummed softly.

"I bet you never expected to be touched like this again," Hans whispered. "You need to remember that you're still alive and that it's okay to feel this way."

Hans backed away, and Malcolm nearly groaned, thinking he was leaving him like this. But Hans slowly undid the buttons of his shirt, parting the white fabric until Malcolm's chest and belly lay bare to Hans's intense scrutiny.

"I'm old," Malcolm said as he reached for his shirt to tug it back into place.

"No," Hans snapped. "You're you, and that means you're just fine." Hans leaned forward and lightly swiped his tongue up Malcolm's belly and around a nipple.

Unable to contain himself any longer, Malcolm lolled his head back and moaned loudly. Damn, that sent a spike of desire racing down his back, making his balls quiver and his cock throb.

"There is nothing you should be ashamed of," Hans said.

"But I'm flabby and…."

Hans sucked at his nipple, and Malcolm completely forgot what else he was going to say. Hell, he might have fucking mewled. He definitely arched his back, hoping for more. Hans had his own ideas about pacing, and Malcolm was quickly becoming impatient.

"Take it easy," Hans soothed and kissed him once again.

Malcolm wanted to get his hands on Hans's skin, and he tugged at his shirt, getting it out of his pants, pulling it upward.

The first skin-on-skin contact sent Malcolm soaring. Hans was heat and energy personified. It radiated from him, surrounding Malcolm with warmth. "Hans… I…."

"You need to take it easy," Hans repeated. "No hyperventilating on me again." He wound his arms around Malcolm's neck and brought their lips together in a kiss that curled Malcolm's toes. More than anything he wanted this to continue.

"I think we need to go somewhere more comfortable," Malcolm said.

Hans stopped and sat up, his weight disappearing. "Malcolm, I don't think that's a good idea." He placed his hand on Malcolm's chest, sending heat through him once again. "I'd love nothing more than to take you up to bed and keep you awake for the rest of the night, but…." Hans paused. "That isn't…. No, that can't happen. Not yet."

"Hans…."

"No," Hans said gently, turning toward the stairs. "I'm guessing that up there in your room is the bed that you and David shared all those years. And I'm also thinking that you and I being together in that bed probably isn't the best idea, right now." Hans slipped farther back, and Malcolm felt the distance in miles rather than inches.

Malcolm pulled his shirt closed over himself and slowly sat up. "I suppose you're right."

"Before you said you needed time and that you wanted to take things slow. That's probably a good idea." Hans stood and tucked in his shirt. "I got a little carried away, and I'm not sorry I did, but stopping now before we get into dangerous territory is for the best." Hans took a deep breath, his full chest filling with air, stretching his shirt.

"Okay, so what next? I'm completely new at all this."

"I'm no expert either, so maybe we do things like people our own ages. We'll take it slower, date, go to the movies or concerts, talk, and see how things work out."

Malcolm nodded as he slowly came back down to earth and everything that had happened that day resettled on him. He'd forgotten all of it for a little while, and while he'd been with Hans, he'd felt light and carefree for a few precious minutes. "Okay."

Hans got his coat and returned to where Malcolm still sat on the sofa. He leaned over him and bent close, kissing him gently. "Why don't you call me in a few days when you've had a chance to think things through and get your feet under you? We can go out for dinner or...." Hans grinned. "Why don't you plan to come to my place on Friday? Do you play poker?"

"I have," Malcolm said cagily.

"Great, you'll need those skills. It'll be fun, and you can see some of what I do for entertainment. I'll call you with details. You won't need to dress like you just came from the office. Comfy casual works for what we'll be doing."

"Okay," Malcolm agreed through dry lips and a dry mouth. He finished buttoning his shirt and stood, following Hans to the door. "I know this seems like a strange time to say this, but sometimes I feel really old. But I don't when you're around."

"Did you with David?" Hans asked.

"No. He always made me feel young and important. I think I forgot what that felt like for a long while." Malcolm went into the entryway and waited for Hans before opening the door to see him off.

"I know this may be hard for you to believe, but I know what you're going through. I didn't lose my partner. Troy is still out there somewhere, probably cheating on his current boyfriend with some guy he hopes will be his next boyfriend. But I lost someone important in my life, and I had to grieve for what I'd lost the same as you have. And for a while I wasn't sure who I was any longer without him."

That sounded so familiar. "It's hard to go from first-person plural to first-person singular," Malcolm said. "In fact, it sucks more than anything I ever went through in my life. But I went through it, and so did you. Most people I know have been through it at one time or another, and I have to say I think it's a huge relief that I might be seeing the light at the end of a very long, dark tunnel."

"I hope so," Hans said and lightly kissed him before stepping out into the cold. Malcolm watched him go. Once Hans was in his car, Malcolm closed the door and turned out the lights, hoping he'd just told Hans the truth. He'd been waiting for some sort of light to shine into his life for so long, and he realized he might have missed it if it weren't for a little luck.

Chapter 5

"I'M LEAVING in a few minutes. Is there anything you'd like me to bring?" Malcolm asked Hans as he pulled his coat out of the closet. Malcolm had been looking forward to this evening the entire week. It had been as hard as he'd thought it would be, but he and the other partners had made progress in restructuring and figuring out how they were going to rebuild what they'd lost as well as position themselves for the future. Replacing Gary had been easier than Malcolm had ever expected. It was figuring out their future direction that had been difficult.

"Just bring yourself over. I have plenty to eat and drink, and I want you to meet my friends," Hans said with a smile in his voice. "It'll be fun, I promise."

He hung up, and Malcolm put on his coat and left the house. An accident at one of the main intersections tied Malcolm up until he could get around it, and he pulled into Hans's driveway ten minutes later. Another car pulled up behind him, and as Malcolm got out, another man approached.

"Sweet car," he said. "I bet it rides like a dream."

"It's comfortable," Malcolm said and followed the man up to the door. He really wasn't sure what to expect, and when he got inside, he was still baffled. Three other guys sat around a table in the living room.

"Malcolm," Hans said happily and leaned in to kiss him. He hesitated for a second, wondering if they should be kissing in front of these guys, but figured Hans knew best.

"Okay, none of that. It's not fair to those of us who seem perpetually single," one of the men said.

"That's Erik. I've known him since I came to this country. And he's only perpetually single because he's a total slut."

"I am not," Erik argued.

"You're a complete manwhore," the man who'd spoken to Malcolm outside said. "And you know it."

"No, he's a slut," Hans said.

"What's the difference?" the man asked as he hung up his coat and took Malcolm's.

"A whore charges and a slut gives it away for free," Hans said, and Erik shook his head.

"That's Chris, and the guy over there not saying much for now is John."

Malcolm shook hands with all of them. "So what are we doing?" For a second he thought poker, but there were no chips. He looked to Hans for guidance.

"Game night," Hans explained.

"Okay. I'm guessing we aren't playing poker because there are no chips or cards."

"Role-playing games," Hans said. "We all used to play Dungeons and Dragons when we were in college, and a few years ago we decided to start playing again. It was really a lot of fun, and we all got to exercise our imaginations. We meet every few weeks."

"I've never played," Malcolm said, taking the seat next to Hans. "I know a few guys who did when I was in school, and they always seemed to enjoy it. But most of my time was spent trying to get into law school and then surviving law school, so I didn't really take part."

"Okay. I need to get set up, and we'll get you initiated into the game," Hans said.

"He's the dungeon master," Erik explained. "Hans is the one who devises the dungeons and directs our play through them. He doesn't actually have any characters in the game."

"I see," Malcolm said.

"Some people use characters and models when they play, but we only use a map based upon what we see and our imaginations about what our characters are doing. It's actually pretty cool."

"We can spread out throughout the room, but most of the guys like sitting at a table, so I use a screen to protect my notes," Hans said as he put up a barrier that was low enough that he could see over it. "Each of the guys has a character or two that they play. Since we're just a few guys, we have extra characters to fill out the exploration party."

"I can give Malcolm one of mine," Erik offered.

"It's not necessary. For this adventure we have a newcomer to our group. I created the character this afternoon, and I've given him some interesting characteristics, though none of you will know what they are because you meet him along the trail. Your female half-elf has decided that he's coming along, and you know how she is." Hans smiled. "That is one horny elf, so you're going to need to watch yourself."

Malcolm chuckled nervously, wondering just what he was getting himself into. Hans handed him a sheet of paper, and he looked it over. Apparently, in the game, he was a human warrior of some sort, with all kinds of various bits of armor and other things that he carried along with him. Malcolm had no idea what some of it was for, and he hoped someone would help him. Hans explained what some of the things were, and then he began setting the scene.

They played for a couple of hours and then broke to eat. Malcolm was surprised at how imaginative the game was and how much he'd gotten drawn in.

"What do you do? In real life, I mean," Erik asked as they gathered around the dining room table. Hans had gotten sandwiches, and there were plenty of snacks as well as beer and soda.

"I'm a tax attorney," Malcolm answered.

"He helped me when I got that letter a few weeks ago," Hans said. "And don't let him be modest. Malcolm is the senior partner at his firm. He's rather brilliant."

"I wouldn't go that far," Malcolm said.

"I would," Hans whispered as he passed right next to him, lightly pressing to Malcolm's backside.

"How is your latest book coming?" John asked as he took his seat once again, watching Hans in a way that told Malcolm there was possibly more interest there than just friends. Hans sat down as well, seemingly not having noticed it at all.

"Very well. I can't quite decide what the volcano is going to do, but it'll come to me."

"I thought this one was under water," John said.

"It is, and so is the volcano."

Hans's eyes gleamed, and Malcolm couldn't wait to hear what Hans came up with. He'd been waiting for this one. He was hoping Hans would let him read it when he was done, but he hadn't been pushing. He hoped Hans would want him to read it.

"Okay, then," John said and returned to his food, but he kept watching Hans like he was the real sustenance.

Malcolm moved a little closer to Hans and wished John would look somewhere else. As time went on, Malcolm became more agitated and actually thought about calling him out.

"What's wrong?" Hans asked when the others went to get seconds.

"Nothing," Malcolm answered too quickly and inwardly chastised himself for the easy giveaway. Hans bumped his shoulder and motioned slightly. "John has a thing for you, and I think I'm jealous."

"John? No way."

Now it was Malcolm's turn to bump Hans, and then he nodded. "He doesn't take his eyes off you."

"Oh," Hans said. "John has never been a huge talker, especially to me, and maybe that explains it."

"He's a nice-looking guy," Malcolm said, and Hans bumped him again.

"There's only one nice-looking guy in this room that I'm interested in." Hans winked, and when everyone returned, they gathered around the table once again and resumed the game.

"THAT WAS lot of fun," Malcolm said a few hours later, once the others had gone. He carried dishes into the kitchen and then grabbed the garbage bag to make a pass through the living room for anything they might have missed earlier.

"It was. I know you probably think it's pretty dorky, but we have fun, and it really helps to keep my imagination sharp. Sometimes I get inspiration for my books from the game, and sometimes we nearly break down into a food fight."

Malcolm picked up the few pieces of trash he found and returned to the kitchen with the last of the dishes from the living room. Hans loaded them into the dishwasher and started it. He placed the last of the leftovers in the refrigerator and closed the door. The kitchen seemed presentable, and Hans sighed before taking Malcolm's arm and leading him out, turning out the lights. "I really didn't invite you over to help with the cleanup."

"I sort of guessed that," Malcolm said and sat on the sofa.

Hans sat next to him. "I wanted you to be able to have a good time and forget about everything that's been going on at the office."

"That's a tall order, but I think you accomplished it. Things are going better than I expected. We're going to offer a partnership to one of our associates, and I've been working on a restructuring plan that I'm going to present to all the partners next week. We need to be more efficient and eliminate as much double work as possible. I also have an idea for bringing in more clients: we offer a reduced rate for our services to new and starting businesses. That way we can help them grow, and once they're successful, they will be full clients and we'll have grown along with them. I need to work out the details with the other partners, but this could provide some potential long-term growth."

"I also think you might consider setting up a literary specialty. It wouldn't be full time, but someone who has expertise in literary contracts and maybe theater could pull that kind of business from a wide area. I had to look for a long time before I found someone with the knowledge I needed, especially when I was starting out, and it would have been nice if that was local. There are a few writers' groups in town. If you had an expert, you could probably arrange to speak at their meetings or something to get the word out."

"I never thought of that."

"Doing things as a service is a great way for people to remember you when they need you and to build goodwill in the community, especially on a personal level," Hans said.

Malcolm nodded slowly. He agreed with that, but at the moment he was much less interested in talking about work than he was in the fact that Hans was sitting right next to him, his intense scent wafting over every now and then, sending Malcolm on little heady loops of desire.

"Malcolm, are you listening to me?" Hans asked, and Malcolm shook his head.

He'd spent his entire week concentrating on what everyone at the firm wanted, listening to suggestions and grief about the office. He'd seen partners act like babies and one throw a temper tantrum and walk out. All he wanted now was a little quiet, and thankfully, when he leaned closer to Hans, resting his head on his shoulder and closing his eyes, he got exactly that.

Hans wound his arm around Malcolm's shoulders, holding him, and they sat quietly as the wind outside picked up, rattling the windows. "We're supposed to get a storm."

Malcolm groaned. "Not another." He hated the thought of shoveling snow, and he wasn't in the mood to drive home through a blizzard.

"Didn't you listen to the weather?" Hans asked.

"Not really. I haven't been home before seven or eight a single night this week, and all that kept me going was the thought of seeing you." Now all that work and those long days seemed to be catching up with him. "I should probably go home now or I'm not going to make it. How bad is it supposed to be?" He really didn't want to think about it.

"Eight inches, give or take," Hans said and tugged Malcolm closer. Malcolm opened his eyes, finding Hans's very close to his. Damn, he loved being looked at like he was important.

"They were that specific?" Malcolm asked, and Hans leaned closer, slanting his mouth over Malcolm's, who promptly forgot about the weather. This was nice, and he was warm and held. He could almost forget about everything else for a while. Hell, maybe that was what he wanted, Hans was a nice guy, and it had been a very long time since he'd been with anyone. Malcolm wasn't into casual sex; he'd given that up quite some time ago. But maybe sex with a friend, someone he liked? That wasn't casual and could be fun. He knew Hans wasn't going to hurt him or be a dick, so.... He pushed the reservations away and wound his arms around Hans's neck, pressing closer, signaling that he wanted more. The wind howled, but that could have been a moan from Hans. He wasn't sure and it didn't matter. The wind couldn't touch him here, in Hans's arms. This was safe and quiet, and his entire being thrummed with energy that had been missing for.... He wasn't going to think it. Instead he decided to let it go and just be. For one night he could do that.

"What was so specific?" Hans asked.

"The amount of snow," Malcolm managed to croak out. "You said eight inches, give or take. I thought you were telling me how much snow we were supposed to get."

"Maybe," Hans whispered and winked.

"You're either naughty or a braggart," Malcolm said, realizing what Hans was insinuating. He sat up and took a deep breath, then stood and looked outside. Snow fell thick, carried and circled by the wind. "I should go if I'm going to make it home." He didn't want to leave, but Hans had not exactly issued an invitation, and he didn't want to assume anything.

Before he could turn around, Hans slid his hands around Malcolm's waist as he pressed to Malcolm's back, hips to his butt, and damn if someone didn't feel like showing off.

"It's supposed to snow for much of the night, and the wind is supposed to be fierce. I checked on my phone, and they're asking motorists to stay off the roads. The winds are higher than they expected, and the storm got here a little sooner."

"I see. So you're saying that we should take their advice."

Hans tugged Malcolm's shirt upward, rubbing his belly in little circles. "We wouldn't want to create a driving hazard, and I certainly don't want you taking any chances on the roads."

Malcolm shivered, but not from the cold, when Hans's hot breath caressed his neck, followed by his lips. Hans shimmied closer, holding Malcolm tightly, his hands wandering upward, and Malcolm leaned back into the embrace, wanting the closeness more than he was willing to admit to Hans or himself. He needed to be touched like an addict needs a fix. He craved it, and Hans gave him what he needed.

"I know what you've been denying yourself," Hans whispered. "I can feel the want seeping from you. Every inch of your skin wants to be caressed."

Malcolm nodded, too into what Hans was doing to bother to put up a front. He gasped when Hans plucked his nipples, over and over, rubbing them until they ached, and he needed more. Malcolm's cock pressed at the front of his jeans, desperate for release, but Hans stayed north of the border.

"Put your head back and give yourself over. I've gone through what you have. I know the fear and the longing. I know how badly you wish you could go back and do it all over again, have one more day. Want nothing more than to be touched and cared for one more time. But you can have that if you allow yourself. Starting over is hard, but you never know what you might find."

"Are you saying you're what I've been looking for?"

"No," Hans breathed and slid his hands over Malcolm's belly and then down his hips to his legs, pressing to his inner thigh and then along his constrained cock and back up to his hip. "Your body is telling me that. Your cock—" He pressed his hand over and along Malcolm's erection before sliding it away again. "—your breathing."

Hans's magic hands slid up to his chest. "Your lips, the way your legs are shaking. It all tells me exactly what you want and need."

"I don't think that's too hard to figure out." Malcolm hoped like hell that Hans didn't stop.

"No. It's more than that. I know that your nipples are really sensitive, and that every time I press my hips to your backside, you press back. When we do go upstairs, I know exactly what you want… what you need."

Malcolm whimpered. "I didn't realize I was an open book. Some lawyer I am."

"This isn't a court, and you aren't trying to hide from me. You want me to know, and that's a really good thing, because if you don't tell me, I can't make you feel the way I want you to."

"Damn," Malcolm breathed. Thinking was the last thing he was able to do at that moment. All he wanted to do was feel, and at that very moment, anticipation and every single one of Hans's touches seemed designed to heighten his desire.

"Exactly," Hans said.

Malcolm expected that they'd go to the bedroom, but Hans stood where he was, in front of the window where they could be seen. Of course, if anyone were to look they wouldn't see much, but after a few minutes, Malcolm began to feel exposed.

"Come with me," Hans whispered just before sucking lightly on his ear.

He stepped away, and Malcolm was suddenly cold and alone. Without thinking he wrapped his arms around him and shivered slightly until Hans unwound his arms and took his hand. He led Malcolm out of the living room, turning out the lights as they went.

The house was dark by the time they reached what Malcolm hoped was Hans's bedroom. Hans flipped a switch, and a soft glow illuminated the rich bed and dresser. Warm fabrics in muted reds covered the chair and draped the windows. The effect was clean and mellow, the perfect environment for sleeping.

Malcolm stood in the doorway, looking at the room while wondering what he was doing here. Suddenly he was standing in another man's bedroom, something he hadn't done in more than twenty years, and the last time had been David's.

"Nothing is going to happen that you don't want to," Hans whispered as he turned around and drew Malcolm to him.

"Have you been with other people since your breakup?" Malcolm asked.

"Yes. At first I went through the 'I'm free' phase, but that didn't last very long, and then I was lonely and tired of it. It's been a while since I was with someone else, and I'm guessing that you haven't been with anyone other than David in twenty-one or twenty-two years."

"You're right. Never wanted anyone else. Sure, I looked at good-looking guys sometimes, but that was all. As far as actually being with someone, it was always David." He hadn't intended the conversation to go to this subject. Malcolm had figured that as long as they kept their conversation on sex or them, he'd be fine, but now that he was face-to-face with being intimate with Hans... he was scared.

"Then like I said, we can take things slow. There's a guest room right across the hall, and you can stay there tonight if that's what you want. No harm... no foul. You won't have anything to apologize for or regret."

Malcolm stepped closer to Hans and gently cupped his cheeks. "I...." God, how did he say that he wanted Hans but was afraid? He wanted to be with Hans, but it felt like he was cheating on David. It was more than just sex, but he also wanted to have sex. It had been since after David's diagnosis. "I do want to be with you."

Hans kissed him, cupping Malcolm's cheeks in return and gently guiding him toward the bed. "Just close your eyes."

"Okay," Malcolm said and let his hands fall to his sides.

Hans kissed him again and then slowly undid the buttons of his shirt, kissing the exposed skin of his neck and shoulders while the fabric fell from his arms and off his hands. "You're sexy, you know that?"

Malcolm shook his head. David had liked his body. They'd been the same age, and they'd grown older and had started the middle-age spread together. They'd also gone to the gym together to stave off some of the inevitable weight gain. "I'm a middle-aged guy who hasn't been to the gym in months."

"Hey. You are the way you are, and that's perfect." Hans kissed his shoulder, and Malcolm sighed. "Time affects all of us, and none of us are the way we used to be."

Malcolm tensed when Hans moved away, but when his chest pressed to him and his bare arms encircled him, Malcolm thought he was going to come on the spot from pure surprised excitement. "I bet you're gorgeous and don't look the way I do."

"So I'm a little younger. This society places way too much emphasis on looks and youth. Intelligence, wisdom, and experience are a lot more sexy." Hans sucked on his ear again, sending shivers through Malcolm. "So just relax and be yourself. You're a successful, confident man who's feeling a little lost and on shaky ground. But that doesn't mean the powerhouse isn't still in there."

"What powerhouse?"

"The one who built his law practice and handled the man from the IRS so deftly he didn't know what hit him. How about the one who's the senior partner at his law firm because he's the most qualified man for the job? Stop putting yourself down and let the real Malcolm out."

"I don't understand."

"All right. Think back to the man you were when you first met David. I'm willing to bet you were cocky, driven, and a bundle of energy." Hans slowly stroked his back. "Don't you want to be that man again?"

"God, yes," Malcolm groaned, pressing closer, needing some friction and stimulation. He kept going from the edge of passion to worry and guilt, and the swings had to stop. It was getting to be too much for him, and he needed to settle his mind.

"Then be that man," Hans told him.

"I think he's gone."

"No, he's still there." Hans pressed Malcolm back until his legs touched the mattress. Hans's kiss was demanding and filled with almost enough energy to shock him. Malcolm felt his reservations slipping away by the second, and he sat down on the edge of the bed and fell backward.

Hans was there instantly, pressing him into the soft mattress. His weight was solid, and Malcolm explored Hans's powerful back, muscles rippling with every movement. Malcolm wanted to take in all of Hans, but at the moment he was sinking deeply into the myriad of sensations running through him.

Malcolm groaned when Hans's weight lifted, and then Hans stepped back. Malcolm was beginning to feel different, the way Hans had said, and he wanted more. He'd been living in a bubble of self-pity and doubt, and it was time for that to stop. Hans pulled off Malcolm's black sneakers and socks, letting them fall to the floor. Then, to Malcolm's surprised delight, he rubbed his feet and up his calves under his pants. Malcolm had no idea that rubbing his legs could be that erotic, but he gripped the bed and held on as Hans ushered in new delights.

When Hans paused again, leaning over him, Malcolm pressed him back and used that opportunity to take him in. Hans was stunning. He'd imagined more than once what was under Hans's clothes, and he'd gotten the chance to feel him a few times, but seeing…. Malcolm knew Hans was a big guy, but he was muscle and light, golden skin set off with a light dusting of reddish-blond chest hair. Pink nipples adorned a full chest, and his arms were thick and corded. Hans wasn't a youngster. His waist was thick—not fat, just thick—with that treasure trail that left Malcolm wondering what it led to. He was more than willing to follow it.

Hans opened his belt and drew it off, then laid it on the chair. He must have known he had Malcolm's undivided attention, and he was going to make the most of it. When he opened the catch on his dark jeans, Malcolm's breath hitched in anticipation. Hans let the pants fall and stepped out of them. Black boxer briefs hugged his legs and thighs. A nearly naked Hans was a sight to behold, and when he stalked closer, reaching for the clasp of Malcolm's belt, Malcolm held his breath, stilling, but his belly fluttered in anticipation. Hans teased the strip of skin above his waist with his fingers, and then he popped the button on his jeans and tugged them open. Hans leaned forward, burying his face in Malcolm's belly, hot breath warming his chilled skin.

"You smell like heaven."

Hans pulled the denim downward. Malcolm lifted his hips, and the jeans slid down his legs. His dark briefs tented, and Malcolm's first reaction was embarrassment, but Hans grinned and nuzzled him, groaning loudly.

Between his arousal and the way Hans licked and sucked at him, his briefs were damp by the time Hans pulled them away and down his legs. Malcolm's self-consciousness had long faded, replaced with sheer lustful desire. Hans had teased and prolonged things to the point where Malcolm's head throbbed. Hans was like a drug. He helped Malcolm scoot back to get comfortable with his head on the pillow. Then he stalked onto the bed, climbing Malcolm as though he were a tree.

"Damn," Malcolm moaned softly, running his fingers over Hans's back. This time he didn't stop, sliding them under the soft cotton fabric to cup Hans's beefy ass. He kneaded the muscle, and it was Hans's turn to moan. That sounded amazing and felt even better. Malcolm loved that he could pull that kind of needy sound out of such a big man.

He pushed the last of Hans's clothes down his legs, and Hans kicked them off before settling back on top of him, sliding his cock along Malcolm's, whose mouth went dry.

"Like that?"

Hans rocked his hips, and Malcolm lightly bit Hans's shoulder to keep from embarrassing himself. He hadn't ever thought he'd feel like this again, and Hans seemed to push all his buttons. So when Hans slid down his body like a snake and without warning sucked Malcolm's cock between his lips, he didn't know how to react. Malcolm placed his hands on Hans's head and thrust upward. He realized too late that he might have surprised Hans, but all Hans did was suck him harder. Now that was hot, "blow off the top of his head" hot. Hans added more pressure, and Malcolm knew he couldn't take much more. The desire and pressure had been building for so long, and with all of Hans's teasing, he wasn't going to be able to prolong things. Not that Hans was taking his time. He seemed to realize that Malcolm was nearing the edge.

He backed off for a few seconds and then sucked Malcolm so hard there was no way Malcolm could hold off any longer. His entire body tingled. Malcolm did his best to warn Hans, but his release came on him so fast that all he could do was grunt before he tumbled over the edge and held on for dear life as months of pent-up energy shot from him.

Warmth and delight hung over him in a way Malcolm had never thought it would again. He stilled and closed his eyes, happy and contented. Hans settled next to him and rolled onto his side, sliding an arm over Malcolm's belly and just holding him.

It took Malcolm more time than he wanted to admit to recover from the release of his life. Getting older definitely sucked, but Hans was patient, and when Malcolm could move again, he opened his eyes and nestled close to Hans, rolling him onto his back.

Hans was like a mountain of muscle. Where he was from, they grew them big and hunky.

"I've wanted to be able to get a good look at you for a while now." Malcolm made little circles on Hans's chest with his fingers, teasing his pink nipples. "You look almost as I imagined."

"Almost?" Hans asked with a lift of one eyebrow.

"Yeah. My imagination didn't quite do you justice." Malcolm let his gaze rake down Hans's belly until it came to rest on his long, thick cock, resting on a blond nest and reaching for Hans's belly button. He leaned over Hans, kissing him as he climbed on top of him. Hans was like a furnace, generating waves of heat that felt amazing. Malcolm stretched out, enjoying as much skin-to-skin contact as possible.

"Fuck," Hans groaned.

Malcolm flexed his hips, sliding Hans along his skin. "Yeah," Malcolm whispered. "You know you aren't the only one who can read others." Malcolm rocked slowly back and forth, and Hans encircled him with his strong, powerful arms, holding him tight. God, it felt so right being held by Hans. Malcolm took in every sensation as he raised his body, straddling Hans and rolling his hips.

Hans's chest expanded with each inhalation, and he stroked Malcolm's thighs as Malcolm continued the slow stroking of Hans's cock. "God," Hans groaned.

"I may be older, but that also means I know a few things." He slid back, wrapping his hands around Hans's cock, stroking him hard and firm. Hans was searingly hot in his hands, and he reveled in it. He rolled his thumb over the head of Hans's cock about every other stroke, applying just the right amount of sensation under the head to send Hans's eyes rolling back into his head.

"Jesus," Hans swore.

"I know." Malcolm was enthralled by Hans's reaction. He stroked harder while cupping his heavy balls. Damn, Hans had been gifted with an amazing cock, and maybe if things worked out, he'd feel it deep inside one day. "You're an incredible man."

"I hope so," Hans said breathily.

"I know so." He twisted his hands, and Hans gasped. "That's it. Give it up for me just like I did you." He locked his gaze with Hans's, knowing that few things were as sexy as looking deep into someone's eyes without reservation. Hans's eyes were like a storm in a blue sky. The blues swirled and deepened the further they went down passion's road. He knew Hans was getting close by the way his eyes widened and from the flush that spread across his cheeks. Then Hans closed his eyes for a few seconds, stilled, and cried out, shaking as he came in ribbons on his belly and chest.

The sight was beautiful, and it was enough to get Malcolm's engine running again. He doubted he'd be able to do anything about it so soon, but that didn't matter. It was just nice to know.

Malcolm leaned forward, capturing Hans's lips in a deep kiss. "I'll go get something," Malcolm said, and Hans groaned and pressed Malcolm back onto the mattress.

"I'll do it. I'll be right back."

Hans climbed off the bed and kissed him before leaving the room. Malcolm stared up at the ceiling, naked on top of the bedding. Now that the passion was spent, he wondered what Hans would want. Not knowing what was expected was strange and made him a little nervous. Before, he'd known what to expect, and things were reasonably predictable. David had been a talker. He loved to lie in bed and talk and talk after sex. Not necessarily about sex, but just talk. Was Hans like that, or was he the kind of guy who cuddled or simply rolled over and went to sleep? Malcolm knew he was probably being dumb and didn't move.

Hans cleaned him gently before going to put back the towel and cloth. When he returned, he jumped up on the bed, bouncing Malcolm and hugging him tightly. Malcolm seemed to have the answer to the rolling over and going to sleep question.

"You want a snack? I can bring you something, and we can watch TV if you want."

"You have a TV in the bedroom?" Malcolm had wanted one, but David was always dead set against it.

"Of course." He got off the bed and opened the cupboard on the far side the room. He brought the remote and pulled back the covers. "Find something you want to watch, and I'll get us a little something."

It seemed naughty to be doing this, but Malcolm got comfortable. When Hans returned with a plate of cheese and two glasses, he set them on the table by the bed, turned out the light, and got under the covers. "I didn't bring anything that would make crumbs," Hans said. He handed Malcolm a glass of ice water and the plate. Then they settled in with Hans holding him close. The only other time Malcolm ever watched television in bed was when he traveled and was staying in a hotel. It was nice, and after drinking the water and eating the cheese, he fell asleep at some point, not even remembering what they were watching.

When he woke a while later, the room was quiet except for Hans's soft snores. Malcolm rolled over, and Hans hugged him close. After that Malcolm let himself be carried away on wings of pleasant exhaustion. The pressure, worries, and everything else could stay in their various boxes for now. He could worry about the repercussions, emotional and otherwise, tomorrow. For now he was happy and felt alive, and that would do.

Chapter 6

"MALCOLM, CAN we talk to you?" Carolyn asked, standing at his corner office door. She had William Fisher with her. He was one of their associates, a bright young attorney with an amazing future.

"Of course," Malcolm said as he did a quick check of his schedule and turned away from his computer. He had a meeting in ten minutes, but Ellen would come get him when the time came. "Please sit down and tell me what's on your mind."

"I've been with the firm for almost five years and…." William turned to Carolyn, who nodded. "I've been told that I'm on the track for a partnership, but I didn't get the opening when Gary left, and I was wondering why. Is there more I need to do?"

"I thought it best that we address this together," Carolyn said.

Malcolm stifled a sigh because each and every associate in the office had come to him at one point or another. They were hungry, smart, and determined. That was why they hired them.

"Nothing has changed as far as your evaluation and prospects. This time around you weren't the top candidate." Malcolm leaned forward. "However, it's important that you understand that the easiest and quickest way to be made partner is to build up your client list to the point where you deserve to be a partner. There aren't a set number of partnership positions in this firm. We can expand them if we need to. Do you understand? You could be a partner in six months as long as you have the client base to support it. Partnerships aren't rewards or based on seniority, but on what you as an attorney can bring to the business." He turned to Carolyn, who nodded her agreement.

"All right," William said.

"We all know you work long hours and bill a lot of hours. That's part of what we look at. The other is your ability to bring in business to the firm. That's where you need to grow. The partners passing work your way isn't what gets you a partnership."

"I understand," William said.

"Excellent. You're a good attorney, and you have the potential to be a great one. That fire you have can get you where you want to go—you just need to aim it in the right direction." The last thing Malcolm wanted to do was discourage him. Most firms pushed and pushed, but the simple truth was that all of their associates worked dang hard and had the fire it took to be a success. But patience was not one of the virtues they generally had.

William left his office, and Carolyn stood to close the door. "Sorry about that," Carolyn said.

"It's not a problem. They all need to know where they stand, and they get antsy when someone else gets what they think they've worked harder than anyone else to get. It's part of what makes them good attorneys. Besides, they need to understand that this isn't a faceless firm, and the last thing we ever want is another situation like what we had with Gary."

"God, no. I did think he might have had some good ideas, but they were never presented in a way that was implementable."

"Exactly." A knock sounded on his door. "That's my next meeting."

Carolyn smiled and got up, passing his clients as they entered the office. Those were his days now—every minute he seemed to have two people who wanted his attention. He hadn't realized how much juggling it would take to do his job well. Maybe he needed to position one of the associates to take over some of his clients so he could have the time he needed for the rest of his job.

"Congratulations, Malcolm," Henry Peterson said as he came into the office. Ellen closed the door behind him, and their meeting began.

AT THE end of the day, Malcolm realized he'd worked through lunch and was starved. He hadn't had a spare minute, and he hoped one part of his job would steady out so he could have a small breather.

"Ellen and I are heading out for the night," Jane said.

"Excellent." He looked up from where he'd been typing frantically. "Come in a minute." She did and closed the door. "I want to put out feelers on getting some help. I need someone I can trust to take over some of my caseload, but it can't be any of our current associates because they don't have specific tax experience."

"What if you mentored one of them?" Jane asked.

"That's possible, but I already know they're clamoring for the more glamourous portions of the law—trial law or corporate. I could get a dozen people to fill those areas."

"All right, but for the record, any of our associates would be a fool not to want to work with you." She turned and left the office as Malcolm's phone rang.

"Malcolm Webber."

"Hi, Malcolm." He'd recognize that happy voice anywhere.

"Hans." He couldn't help smiling.

"Is it a good time to call?"

"Yes. I'm just finishing up and getting ready to go home." He was suddenly very tired, and his mind wandered to how Hans looked lying naked on the bed instead of the e-mail he was trying to compose.

"Do you have plans for Saturday?" Hans asked. "It's been snowing, and I was wondering if you'd like to go skiing. There's a great resort a few hours away. We could go up there and stay the night, ski—spend some time outdoors during the day and in front of the fire at night."

"Skiing," Malcolm asked. "I haven't done that since I was in college." And he'd fallen on his ass more times than he could count and hadn't gone back again.

"Then it's time. Come with me. We can have a lot of fun."

Malcolm hated the thought of saying no and sounding like a killjoy. "All right," he answered a little fearfully. The nights in front of the fire part sounded really nice. He wasn't at all sure about the skiing and cold part. "I wasn't very good back then."

"Don't worry, I'll teach you. I promise you'll have a good time." Hans sounded so happy that Malcolm didn't want to rain on his parade. "I'll go ahead and make the reservations and get lift tickets. We'll need to rent you equipment, but we can take care of that once we get there."

"What time do we need to meet?"

"How about I pick you up at your place on Saturday morning? We can head on up and ski in the afternoon. I'll make us dinner reservations as well. It'll be wonderful. I promise. How's your week going?"

"Pretty well. It's been very busy, and I haven't had more than a few minutes to breathe in days."

"Then some fun is in order for this weekend. Leave it up to me, and I'll pick you up on Saturday." Hans said he'd call soon and hung up. Malcolm put his phone on his desk and went back to work on his e-mail. He didn't have much time to worry about the weekend when he was so busy.

Malcolm worked later than he intended and didn't get home until after eight. He'd stopped on the way home for Greek takeout and ate it in front of the television. When he couldn't keep his eyes open any longer to watch the show, he turned it off and cleaned up his mess before heading upstairs. Like he'd done a million times before, he showered and went through his nightly routine before crawling into his side of the bed.

Of course, when he wanted to sleep, he couldn't, no matter how tired he was. Malcolm kept wondering what in the hell he was doing. He rolled over, facing David's empty side of the bed. "I know you think I'm crazy for holding on like I am. You always said that when something happened to you, you wanted me to be happy. But am I doing the right thing?" Of course he didn't get an answer. David wasn't there, and no amount of talking in the dark was going to get him answers. "I like Hans. I really do. He's fun and he understands how I feel. Let's face it, the guy is really smart, but how can I keep up with him?"

In his mind he could hear David laughing at him. Throughout their twenty years together, David had been the adventurous one. He liked to try new things and booked them on cruises and vacations to exotic places. Malcolm went along and always had a great time. So why would things be any different now? He was out doing new things, only with Hans instead of David. Maybe he was getting old, but he didn't have to act like it. That was for damn sure.

The next few days were even busier, and by Friday night, Malcolm fell into bed, sleeping through the night and not waking until the doorbell rang, accompanied by insistent pounding on his front door. Malcolm checked the clock and jumped out of bed. He hadn't overslept in a decade at least. He pulled on a pair of sweatpants and hurried down the stairs.

Hans's expression was a mixture of confusion and anger. "Come in. I'm sorry," Malcolm said as he ushered Hans inside. "I worked really late last night so I could have the weekend, and it looks like I slept through part of it. Let me go up and get dressed so we can go." He got Hans inside and closed the door before hurrying toward the stairs.

"Malcolm, it's only nine in the morning. I called an hour ago to see if you wanted to get breakfast before we left, and you didn't answer. I got a little worried and called again. When you didn't answer the second time, I thought something was wrong and headed over."

"I'm fine. Just sleeping in a little longer than usual." He wasn't sure if he should be angry that Hans was concerned that he was so old he'd keel over or pleased with his concern. He decided to go with the latter because he didn't need any reminders of getting older. "There's coffee if you want it." He always set the pot to start in the morning.

"Take your time," Hans said, and Malcolm climbed the stairs and set out warm clothes before starting the shower in the master bathroom. He loved this room with its huge shower, natural tiled walls, and under-floor heating. It was the perfect bathroom. Malcolm stepped under the water, washing quickly and then rinsing off before turning off the water. He didn't look at himself in the mirror as he finished up. There was no need. He knew what he looked like, and he didn't need to see the silver around his temples or the gray on his chest.

When he stepped out of the room in a towel, he found Hans sitting on the edge of his bed, staring at him. The heat in that gaze was enough for Malcolm to forget all those thoughts about getting older. And when Hans smiled and leered at him, Malcolm nearly looked around to find out who else was in the room. Hans was looking at him. Why, Malcolm had no idea, but he was, and there was nothing sexier than being the object of someone else's undivided attention. Hans didn't move other than to sip from his mug, but Malcolm felt his gaze on him every second. Malcolm dropped the towel and began to get dressed. He was excited beyond belief and wondered if he could entice Hans into bed. Hell, maybe they wouldn't actually have to go anywhere.

He put on his pants and shirt before pulling on a sweater, then turned to look at Hans. He had thought ahead far enough to pack his bag. "I just need to get my kit." He went into the bathroom. "You don't have to stick close—I'm not going to make a run for it or something." He got what he needed, then returned to the bedroom.

Hans sat in his same place. "I like watching you."

"Why?" Malcolm put his kit in his bag and then looked down at himself. "It's not as though I'm statueworthy or something."

"That's a strange thing to say. Where is that coming from?"

Malcolm sighed a little. "It's how David and I met the very first time. We didn't date or go out then, but it was the mideighties, and I was desperately trying to get through law school and needed money. I met David when he and I were in the same art class."

"You took art?"

"No. David was exploring his interests at the time, and he'd signed up for a drawing class. And I was the live model. I remember walking into that class and taking off my shirt."

"Did you get naked?"

"Not right away, but as the class progressed, I did." Malcolm smiled and went to the dresser, then pulled open the bottom drawer. He took out a framed picture and handed it to Hans. "This is one of the drawings David did of me." It was only a torso, and Malcolm knew it wasn't particularly adept. That class had apparently ended David's thoughts of being an artist.

"Did you date him?"

"Oh, God no. I was just the model in the class, and while I noticed David because he was handsome, I never approached him, and once I posed nude, I found it best to keep some distance from the students. It made things easier. I met David again almost a decade later, and after we went out, he gave me that, and we shared a huge laugh. He told me that he'd always remembered me." Malcolm sat on the edge of the bed, holding the drawing to him as he fell into a sea of memories and found himself smiling. "He would try just about anything. Apparently at one point he was interested in sculpture. Thankfully, none of those efforts survived. There are pictures of animals that look like they have three heads and six legs. He said they were supposed to be representational. I told him I thought that had proved that he'd tried LSD, and he smacked me on the shoulder and stuck his tongue out. To this day, I don't know if I was right or not. There were few things in his life that David didn't talk about, and that was one."

"You think he did?" Hans asked.

"I don't know. Something changed him between the time we first met and when we got together again. He was more serious and…. It's hard to say. When we reconnected, he was a social worker and I was a hotshot young attorney ready to take on the world." Malcolm stood up and put the drawing away. "Why don't we get going?" He needed to stop this trip down memory lane or he'd talk forever, and that wasn't something he needed to do to Hans.

"All right." Hans grabbed Malcolm's bag and kit and left the room, heading down the stairs. "You're going to need good gloves, heavy insulated ones. I don't suppose you have snow pants or something like that."

"I'll have to see." David had been an outdoorsy guy, so maybe he'd had something. Malcolm had given away most of David's things, but after he'd gone through everything, he'd found a large hanging bag of winter gear in the basement, and he'd left it there.

Malcolm got going. He found his gloves, then went into the basement and unzipped the hanging bag in the storeroom. There were a couple of David's coats and a full-body snowsuit. Malcolm wondered how old it was and then toed off his shoes. He heard footsteps on the stairs as he pulled on the suit. It was a little snug around the middle, but it fit okay.

"How old is that?"

"I don't know. I remember David wearing it years ago, but I haven't seen it again in a while. I'm surprised he still had it. The legs and arms are long enough, so it seems to fit." He turned around, and Hans looked him over. Then he unzipped it and stepped out before pulling on his shoes.

"That should be good," Hans said as Malcolm motioned toward the stairs.

"Is there anything else? I'm assuming the boots will be rented with the skis, and I have a hat."

"I brought an extra pair of ski goggles for you. Some guys just wear sunglasses, but goggles are really best. There can be a lot of snow and things that get thrown up, and you don't want any of it in your eyes." Hans left to make a trip to his car, and Malcolm checked through the house, locking up the doors and turning out the lights. Then he joined Hans in his green Toyota Camry, which seemed stuffed to the gills, and they started out.

"How did you and David reconnect?" Hans asked as they approached the highway toward downtown. From the brochure Hans handed him, they were headed to Devil's Snow Mountain, north of Madison.

"David worked for a private nonprofit organization that helped families who were falling through the government cracks. They were being sued, and they needed an attorney. The firm I worked for at the time had been asked to help them on a pro bono basis, and I was assigned. David wasn't my contact, but as I was doing the work, I stopped by one afternoon to ask some questions, and I saw David with a group of kids. He was surrounded by them, and each one was clamoring for his attention. I watched him as he worked with them. When he saw me, he smiled, and then he recognized me and waved. My heart did this somersault, and that was it. I knew I wanted to get to know him better."

"Did you win the case?"

"Yes. At the time the plaintiffs were accusing the organization of not doing enough to help them. It was really a stupid argument, and they had no chance of succeeding. The organization was private and not under any obligation to help anyone. The woman had been evicted and was blaming them. I got the case thrown out easily, and once I was done, I asked David if he'd go out with me. On our second date he gave me the drawing I showed you. He said he'd always remembered me and wished he'd been smart enough back then to ask me out."

Hans made the transition west, and they zoomed out of town. It was freeing in a way to be away from home and going to a place he'd never visited before.

"Sometimes the memories seem like a huge weight pressing down on me," Malcolm said.

"How so?" Hans asked.

"Well, it's like I'm supposed to remember everything so I don't forget David. But each day something fades a little, though I keep working harder and harder to keep the memories focused and sharp. I don't want to forget David, but the more I try, the more he slips through my fingers, so I try even harder. Then of course there are other times when I realize that David will always be with me and that I'm not going to forget the life we had." He inhaled deeply and let it go. "Things will change and my life will be different, and that's okay." Malcolm sat back and stopped talking about David. He'd done that enough for one day. "How long have you been skiing?"

"I learned years ago. You know I grew up in Denmark, and Nordic sports were part of being a kid there. Winter lasts a long time, so we made the most of it. I cross-country skied, but that's basic transportation. I tried ski jumping for a while, and that was a rush. I like to think I outgrew that. Now I ski downhill. I used to snowboard as well, but after an injury and a broken arm that meant I had trouble writing for over a month, I decided the thrill wasn't worth the risk. You said you skied in college."

"Yeah. I had friends who skied, and they took me with them a few times. I wasn't very good and spent most of the time in the wedge, looking like a complete dork on the bunny hill. I managed to learn how to fall and did that a lot. But in the end I gave up and let the guys have their fun. It wasn't worth slowing them down and keeping them off the larger hills, which was what they really wanted." Malcolm shrugged and looked out at the snow-covered landscape.

"You're going to have fun today. I promise. We'll take the time to show you how to ski properly, and you'll be having fun in no time."

Malcolm nodded, but he wasn't so sure about that. However, he wasn't going to complain. Hans had gone through some trouble to arrange all this, and how long could they stay outside in the cold anyway?

THEIR ROOM at the resort was ready for them, and they went right to it. Hans had reserved a deluxe suite, and it not only had a fireplace but a hot tub as well. Both of which had sexy possibilities.

"Why don't you get changed, and we can go down, get our lift tickets, and rent you some equipment?"

Hans was already getting into his gear, so Malcolm did the same. He felt a little like the abominable snowman wearing all those layers, but Hans said he'd need it. They trudged out to the ski area and got Malcolm's equipment and boots.

Hans looked amazing in a ski outfit that matched his skis. He helped Malcolm get his on and adjusted. Then he helped him glide out across the basin toward the rope lift to the top of the bunny hill.

From the bottom, it looked tall. "You're going to be fine," Hans said. "Don't grab the rope all at once, or you'll fall. Think of it like the clutch on a car and let it get you moving a little before you completely grab hold."

"Okay." Malcolm watched Hans, and then he gave it a try, thankful there weren't too many people behind him. Of course he fell, and Hans came around to help him.

"Try it again."

Hans held his poles, and Malcolm made sure his skis were straight and tried for the rope again. This time he managed to stay upright, and the rope pulled him up to the top. As soon as he let go, he wondered what to do and instantly fell one more time. Hans helped him up and got his poles for him.

"You made it, and that's what counts."

Malcolm wasn't so sure, but he wasn't going to give up either. "What do I do now?" Little kids zoomed around him, and Malcolm stifled a groan, but he swallowed the remark that rose to his lips.

"You remember the wedge? It's a way of controlling your speed," Hans said. "But you have little control and everyone falls on their butt. The other way is to just go down the hill, but if you go straight, you go too fast and can't control it. The trick is to weave back and forth, and to do that you simply shift your weight a little. I'm going to show you. Don't do it until I come back up. We'll work together, okay?"

Malcolm nodded, and Hans went down the hill like it was nothing. Malcolm watched the way he moved and began mimicking him without going down. He watched as Hans slid over to the rope, and up he came as easily and gracefully as anything Malcolm had ever seen.

"Do you want to give it a try?" Hans asked.

"I'll give it a shot." He moved into position and stopped. How on earth was he supposed to do this?

"Just a second. Make sure your skis are straight and don't cross the tips. Also look where you want to go. Your body will tend to take you there."

Malcolm lifted his gaze toward the lodge and closed his eyes. Maybe if he wished hard enough he'd magically transport inside in front of a fire. When he opened them he was still outside and swore under his breath before starting down the hill. He turned to the right, and it worked. So he tried going left, went ass over teakettle, and ended up lying flat in the snow. His skis came off and continued happily down the hill. Hans schussed up to him and helped him up. Malcolm brushed himself off and managed to walk the rest of the way down the hill to retrieve his skis.

"That was good."

"Huh?" he asked skeptically, as eight-year-olds called to their parents to watch them zoom by him. This was totally embarrassing.

"You turned. Let's go back up and try again." He led the way over to the rope, and Malcolm went back up. This time he managed to make it down the hill without falling, which he counted as a victory.

"Go on and catch the lift to the bigger runs," Malcolm said. "I know that's where you'd like to be. Let me stay here for a little while and see if I can figure this out."

"You sure?"

"Yeah. Go and have fun." Malcolm caught Hans's eye and smiled. Hans was so excited, and Malcolm was determined not to make a complete fool of himself. When Hans slid away to the main lifts, Malcolm went up the rope pull. He did it again and again, slowly getting the hang of things. When Hans returned, he showed him what he'd figured out and how he could actually make it down the hill, turning back and forth.

"See, I knew you could do it," Hans said when he reached the bottom. "The last part is to use your legs as shock absorbers. Bend them so when you go over a bump, you don't shake your entire body."

Hans showed him, and Malcolm went down one more time, feeling confident.

"That's it. You have the basics. Now let's go have some fun."

"Okay, where?" Malcolm asked, and Hans looked at the lift that went halfway to heaven. "You have to be crazy. You want me to go all the way up there?"

"Yeah. There are easier runs off to the side. We'll go down those. They're faster than this one and longer, but not as steep as that one."

Hans went over, and Malcolm reluctantly followed, wondering if he was putting his life in Hans's hands.

They rode up in the lift together. That part he liked. Hans pointed things out, and the two of them held hands like naughty teenagers. Hell, if he'd had his way they might have done other things like teenagers, but they ended up at the top before Malcolm really knew it. With a stroke of luck, Malcolm was able to get off without falling and followed Hans as they skied down a trail to a lower portion of the mountain.

"This is it," Hans said, and Malcolm looked down toward the bottom of the cliff they were standing on top of. Okay, it wasn't that steep or tall, but dang…. "Just use your skis to control your descent and go from side to side, and you'll be awesome. It's just a little steeper than the hill you were just on and only a bit longer. I'll stay behind you and watch."

"Okay," Malcolm said and pushed off at an angle. He turned and started going straight down, picking up speed. He turned again and slowed. That was awesome. So he turned back and was going straight downhill. This time he kept going and went faster and faster. He was now too scared to turn, so he hoped like hell everyone was out of the way. Malcolm was doing great, and the bottom of the hill was in sight. He adjusted his skis, and his legs flew out from under him. He did his best to go down onto his butt but ended up on his side, rolling like a log. All he could think to do was keep his arms in because he didn't want to snap them. He lost both skis, and his poles went flying.

Malcolm was never so grateful to come to a stop in his life. The first thing he did was take inventory. His legs and arms worked. His head wasn't aching and didn't seem to have been split open. His face was cold as hell, but that was because his head was in the snow. He lifted his neck and slowly got his knees under him.

"Are you hurt?" Hans asked as he raced up to him.

"I don't know. I don't think I broke anything."

"I'll get your stuff," Hans said, and Malcolm secretly hoped he couldn't find everything. Of course, he brought the skis and poles over. "You were doing great until you crossed your skis."

"You mean until I rolled down the hill like a lump and landed in a pile?" He looked up toward the top as they got their things and moved out of the way.

"I'll help you get the skis on, and then we can try it again."

"Oh God," Malcolm groaned under his breath. Hans helped him with the skis, and they glided over to the lift once again, waiting in line for their turn. Malcolm was starting to wonder if hell was actually in an upward direction, especially the closer they got to the top once again.

Somehow, by sheer will he got to the bottom without falling. Hans was thrilled, but Malcolm's hip was aching. He didn't want to disappoint Hans, so he followed him up again, and after a few more runs, he was getting better and falling less.

"Are you ready to warm up?" Hans asked.

Malcolm nodded, and they skied over to the lodge, took off their skis, propped them in the place provided, and went inside. It was warm, and they were lucky enough to find empty chairs in the large hotel lobby, near the fireplace. A huge fire burned in the hearth, and Malcolm sighed as he took off his boots and put his feet up.

"Did you have a good time?" Hans asked, scooting his chair close enough that he could touch Malcolm's hand.

"It was different than what I remembered. I actually did it," Malcolm said and shifted slightly in the chair. His hip ached, and the pain was increasing. But he didn't want to dampen Hans's fun, so he kept quiet. "When is dinner?"

"We have a reservation for seven. That's an hour and a half from now. Are you warmed up enough for another run?" Hans was clearly anxious to get back out.

"Not really." He was thawing out, but the thought of going back into the cold made him shiver. "If you want to go back out, you can, and I'll head down to the room." Malcolm levered himself onto his feet. He tried not to make a face, but his hip ached something awful. "I'm fine," he lied when Hans helped him up.

"No, you're not." Hans picked up his boots. "I'll get the skis and things." He went back to the door they'd come in, and Malcolm got his boots and slowly walked to the elevator and then down to their room.

Once inside, Malcolm carefully stripped off his snow gear and sweater. Then he pulled off his jeans and groaned. His right hip was turning purple. He'd bruised himself really badly. Ice was probably best, but the thought of being cold again was too much. Malcolm lay back on the bed, resting his hip and back, breathing deeply and trying to relax. He closed his eyes.

Hans came in carrying everything with him. He set the skis out on the balcony and came back in. "Tired?"

Malcolm tugged at the band of his boxer briefs, and Hans hissed. "Why didn't you say something?"

"Because I didn't want to stop you from having a good time." He lay still as Hans gently touched his hip.

"Is it broken?"

"No. I think I just bruised it. I'll take something for the pain and inflammation and get dressed in a little while." He sighed as Hans sat on the edge of the bed. "I don't want you to stop having fun. If you want to go back out after dinner, please do."

"Nope. After dinner we'll get you comfortable and see what we can do to make you forget about your hip."

Malcolm wasn't sure he wanted to move at all. Hans brought him his kit and a glass of water. Malcolm took a couple of ibuprofen and then lay back again to wait for them to kick in. Half an hour later, the pain began to recede, and Malcolm moved slowly, getting dressed and waiting for Hans to do the same. Then they left the room and gingerly went down for dinner.

In the dining room, he and Hans were shown to their table. Malcolm put the injury out of his mind as best he could.

"I'm sorry you're hurt."

"I think I was starting to get the hang of it," Malcolm said before ordering a glass of wine. Outside the huge windows that lined one wall, skiers continued going up and down the slopes under powerful lights that shone over the entire area. "After dinner if you want to go back out, I think you should. I'll rest in the room for a while, and when you come back in we can spend some time in the hot tub."

Hans was obviously torn and said nothing, but Malcolm knew he'd come here to ski and have a good time. Sitting with Malcolm in the room or in front of the fire wasn't what an active guy like Hans was interested in.

"I'll be fine." Hans reached across the table. "I came here to be with you." He squeezed Malcolm's hand. "Have you decided what you're going to have for dinner?"

"I'm thinking of the chicken." He'd already decided to have something simple. That was usually safest. The food coming out of the kitchen looked good and made Malcolm hungry. "How about you?"

"I was thinking steak," Hans said with a grin. When the server brought their drinks, they placed their orders.

"What else do you like to do with your time besides ski?" Malcolm asked before sipping his wine.

"I'm certified for open-water and deep-water diving. I love riding horses and racing dune buggies, though I haven't done that in a while. I used to have my own buggy but gave that up a few years ago. So I took up sailing. I'd love to be part of a competitive team, but that hasn't happened yet. I think I might be a little too old, but I'd really like to explore it."

"You probably live in the wrong place for that. Don't most of the races take place off the East and West Coast?"

"There are plenty of Great Lakes races."

Hans sipped his water, eyes lighting up with excitement. Malcolm drank most of his glass of wine. Then he flagged down the server for another. There was no way in hell he could keep up with

Hans. Scuba diving, competitive sailing, racing. Heck, he went skiing with him once and hurt himself. If he tried the other things Hans did, he'd probably end up dead. Getting drunk wasn't going to help, but the warmth of the wine felt good.

"How do you get to be on one of those teams?" he asked Hans.

"Sometimes they have calls for members, but mostly you have to know someone and get a reputation within the community. I'm just starting out, so a top race team is probably out of the question, but I think it would be an awesome challenge and make the premise for a really good book. I love to include my activities in my books. The things that happen have to feel real even if they aren't possible outside of my imagination."

"I never thought of that."

"In my next book, I'm going after Atlantis. So many other writers have tackled the same idea, so I want to try something different. There's a team who believes they have actually discovered Atlantis, close to where Plato described it. Believe it or not, they think it's in Spain, and there is evidence of a great wall of water that would have covered the city. The whole thing is really cool, and I'd like to explore that in a book. Of course, there will be more to it than that, and I'll glam it up a bit, because there has to be something there that needs to be found to save the world from complete destruction."

"Will you go to Spain?" Malcolm asked.

"I went last year to see the location. It doesn't look like much, but the contours of the land are interesting, and satellite photographs show the entire layout. So I can probably work from what I have. But I may need to go back. Sometimes I don't know until I start writing. I plot out the books to a point, but then I need to write to see what else I need."

Malcolm shifted in his chair, his hip aching once again. The painkiller was only doing so much. Thankfully the server brought their meals. They continued talking while they ate, but Malcolm's mind kept wandering to his hip and the ache that didn't seem to go away. Once dinner was over, Malcolm had a difficult time getting up.

His hip didn't want to move, which was just awesome. They went back to the room, and Malcolm lay on the bed while Hans hovered.

"Go on and ski for a while if you want. The slopes are open for another few hours, and you may as well have some fun," Malcolm told him.

"Are you sure?"

"Yeah. Go have some fun, and I'll be right here waiting for you." He felt so damn old at the moment.

"Are you sure it's just a bruise?" Hans asked, and Malcolm nodded. "You really want me to go?"

"You want the truth? I want you to stay right here with me. But I know you want to be out there having fun. You spent most of the time we were out there with me, and you need some time to let loose. I'm not going anywhere, though if I can get my hip to cooperate, I might see if there's a chair by the fire."

"If you're sure," Hans said, biting his lower lip. He was clearly conflicted.

"There's no use having both of us cooped up in here. Go and have fun. I'll go to the lodge and watch for you." Malcolm got up, hobbled over to Hans, and closed him in his arms. "I mean it." He kissed him, and Hans hugged him tight, deepening the kiss and groaning softly. The pain in Malcolm's hip receded as he thought of fun things they could do right in the room.

"I'm going to get my things," Hans said, and Malcolm released him and let him get ready before heading slowly down to the lodge. He had trouble finding a seat but managed one near the windows. It wasn't close to the fire, but he had an ottoman to put his feet up on, and one of the hotel staff offered him a plaid blanket. He put it over his legs, ordered a hot chocolate with a splash of rum, and sat back to relax and watch outside.

He saw Hans wave as he passed, and he waved back, following him with his eyes until Hans melded into the line waiting for the lift.

"Do you mind if I join you?" a handsome man about Malcolm's age asked.

Malcolm motioned to the other chair. "That would be nice."

"I saw you with your friend." He smiled and signaled the waiter, ordering a martini. "Have you been dating long?"

Malcolm paused for a second. "A few weeks. He's an active kind of guy." *And I'm feeling every bit my age at the moment.* He kept that last part to himself.

"I see that."

He grinned wryly, and Malcolm wondered what that was all about.

"Why aren't you out there with him?" The server brought their drinks, and he took a sip. "I'm James, by the way."

"Malcolm." He sipped from his glass. "Are you here with someone?"

"Yes. Mine's out on the slopes as well. He'll spend the evening on the slopes and then be raring to go all night long." James had this wicked look. "That's him there," James said.

Malcolm followed his gaze and blinked a few times. The guy looked like he was fifteen. That was an exaggeration, but he was young.

"He's gorgeous, and at that age they have so much energy."

"Were you out skiing?" Malcolm asked.

James shook his head. "Good God, no. I'd break my neck." He leaned forward. "Gregory loves to go skiing and all that. He's as active as they come, and I've stopped trying to keep up. So I take him where he wants to go, have my own fun while he's out, and then when he comes in, we get to play." James sat back, as happy as anything.

"What do you talk about?" Malcolm asked.

James laughed. "A lot of talking isn't usually what we do when we're together."

"How long have you been seeing each other?" Malcolm understood pretty clearly what type of relationship James was talking about.

"Four months now, and things seem to be working out fine." James sipped his drink, looking out the window. After a few moments he waved and raised his glass. "He makes me feel young. They all do."

"All?" Malcolm asked.

"Sure. I have no illusions. Gregory and I do things together, and I pay for them. He likes going on ski trips and taking vacations to the Caribbean, and I like how he makes me feel."

"But how long will he stick around?"

James shrugged and sipped from his glass once again. "They last about a year, and then they move on, and I find someone new."

"So you don't expect anything long term?" Malcolm asked.

"No," James said and shook his head. "I have my eyes open, and so does he. I like Gregory—he's a nice guy and we get along. But he has his interests and I have mine." James turned away from the window. "How long do you think things will last between you and your guy? He's out there and you're in here."

Malcolm had no idea. He liked Hans and hoped the feeling was mutual. Malcolm wasn't interested in a relationship like the one James had. Not that there was anything wrong with it as long as no one got hurt, but that wasn't his way. "I don't know." Malcolm wondered if he should have gutted it out and gone skiing once again with Hans. This whole conversation made Malcolm very uncomfortable. "I think that's part of what makes relationships exciting."

"I didn't mean to upset you," James said, and Malcolm realized some of his worry must have made it into his voice. "Things are different for different people, of course."

"I know that," Malcolm said as lightly as he could, turning to look out the window. He didn't see Hans, not that he'd expected to. It just would have been nice. He needed to change the subject. "What do you do?"

"I have my own business," James said. "You?"

"I'm a... the senior partner with Warren, Hanlan, and Webber in Milwaukee." They hadn't decided if they were changing the name. At the moment the name of the firm was what people remembered, and even with Gary gone, the name on the masthead was for his father.

"I'm familiar with them. They did great work for an acquaintance of mine, Marshall Gunderson."

Malcolm nodded. He was familiar with the client, but he said nothing. He wasn't going to divulge anything he shouldn't.

"Your firm was great when someone tried to steal his copyrights." James reached into his pocket and pulled out a card.

Malcolm took it and instantly recognized the name. James McLelland. His firm was a huge manufacturer of industrial lift equipment.

"I believe there's something you can help us with. Do you have a card?"

Malcolm pulled out his wallet and handed James one of his cards. "Call me directly, and we can talk over what you need in a more private setting."

"I'd appreciate that," James said and placed the card in his pocket.

Warm hands gently slid along Malcolm's shoulder. "Are you feeling any better?" Hans asked from behind him.

"A little," Malcolm answered and turned, looking into Hans's warm eyes. "Hans, this is James. His boyfriend was out skiing as well, and we were keeping each other company." Hans came around and sat on the arm of the chair.

"It's nice to meet you," Hans said, shaking James's hand before he turned back to Malcolm. "We should get back to the room before that hip stiffens up too much."

"It was great talking to you, James. Give me a call next week." Malcolm shook James's hand, surprised at how limp his handshake was, but he didn't react to it.

"I will," James said as Malcolm removed the blanket from over his legs and stood up.

He still hurt, and he had no doubt he'd be stiff as a board come morning, but for now he felt okay, and he wanted to enjoy the rest of their evening. They made their way to the elevators and then up to the room on the second floor. Hans opened the door, and Malcolm went inside.

"Get undressed, and we'll spend some time in the hot tub. That should loosen you up a little before we go to bed."

Hans put his gear on the balcony, and Malcolm heard the spa motor's low whir. He began undressing, and Hans turned out the lights so that it was dark.

"You want me to go out there naked?" Malcolm asked when Hans stripped off and turned out the last lights in the room. Hans got some towels, and then he opened the glass door and stepped into the whirlpool.

"It's perfect," Hans said softly, and Malcolm followed his lead, closing the door and sinking into the hot, swirling water.

At first his hip ached, but then it loosened up and the pain slowly melted away. The heat felt good, and Hans's hands on his legs felt better, especially when Hans shifted between them, gently wrapping Malcolm's legs around his waist.

Malcolm was hard enough to pound nails, and when Hans leaned back a little, his cock slid against Hans's lower back. That was heavenly, and he held on to Hans, resting his head on his shoulder, pressing his chest to Hans's back. "You feel so good."

"So do you," Hans said, moving away slowly and sitting back down. Hans tugged Malcolm to him, and as Malcolm shifted, Hans supported some of his weight until Malcolm straddled Hans's lap, sitting across his legs. "Be careful. I don't want this to hurt," Hans whispered into Malcolm's ear as he settled a big hand on each of Malcolm's cheeks.

"It doesn't," Malcolm moaned as Hans ghosted his fingers over his opening. Malcolm held Hans, groaning and shaking as Hans teased him with his fingers while Hans's cock throbbed between them.

Damn, this was sexy, and Malcolm kissed Hans hard as he teased his opening and then slipped the tip of his finger inside. Malcolm gasped, holding his breath. It had been a long time, and being intimate like this was mind blowing. Malcolm had never thought of himself as a sex outdoors kind of guy, but at this moment he didn't care about anything other than Hans's hands on his ass and the way he kissed and sucked at his neck.

"I want you, Malcolm. I want to be with you."

Malcolm tried to answer, but all that came out was gibberish that morphed into another moan as Hans sank his finger a little deeper, rubbing that spot inside that made Malcolm's eyes roll into his head.

"Lie back," Hans whispered, and Malcolm slid off his lap and down into the water. Hans grabbed a few towels and spread them out along the side of the tub. Then he lifted Malcolm partially out of the tub, supporting his hips and butt, lifting him until his cock stood straight out of the water. "Damn, that's pretty." Hans took him deep and hard, bobbing his head, the water sloshing around him.

"Hans, I...." Malcolm's words tapered off to a hum and then silence. He knew they had to be quiet because there were other rooms nearby, but this was too damn much. Hans stroked up his belly and chest and then slipped a finger between his lips. Malcolm sucked it because he needed something to do with his mouth, but if Hans kept that up he was in danger of losing a finger. Hans had the ability to make him forget. His tongue and lips, the magic he made with them, sent all other thoughts from his head.

Every cell in his brain screamed at the same time, and his body tingled from head to toe. Each stroke of Hans's lips sent a quiver through him. Wet heat, pressure, soft yet firm touches, had him on edge and kept him there. Malcolm wanted to come more than anything, but Hans held him just this side of release for what seemed like hours.

"I can read exactly what you want," Hans said when he came up for air. "I told you before that I can read you like a book, and I love it. You are so incredible." Hans stood, his nakedness shining in the darkness. He leaned over him and captured Malcolm's lips. "I want you to be happy. That's the one thing I want more than anything."

"Why? What's so special about me?"

"You keep asking things like that, when I keep wondering what you see in me. I'm just a writer. You fight for people and try to bring some justice to this world. I know it doesn't always work out that way when you practice law, but I know that's why you went into this profession."

Malcolm shivered as the chill in the air cooled his skin. "I'm not all that special," he said.

Hans slithered down his chest, kissing a trail down his belly, and then gripped his cock firmly. "I wish I knew where all this came from." Hans grinned. "But I'm going to find out." He sucked at the head and then slowly sank his lips down Malcolm's shaft. Heat and cold mixed on his skin, and Malcolm gave himself over to the intense sensation, pushing the cold away, thrusting upward. The water sloshed, and Hans drove him wild. Hans was right there, taking what he had to give until Malcolm was all in. Hans pulled back, gripping him hard and stroking fast. Malcolm lost control, and within seconds the world had narrowed to Hans and his touch. Malcolm lifted his head, catching Hans's gaze, and that did it. His control snapped and he came. Malcolm had no idea how much noise he made, and he didn't care. Hans guided him into the warm water, and he leaned his head back, closed his eyes, and breathed slowly, trying to recover from having his mind completely blown.

"You didn't get hurt, did you?"

Malcolm chuckled. "God, no," he said between breaths. "Was I too loud? Did I scare the neighbors?" he whispered.

"You were amazing, and the neighbors have been making plenty of noise of their own."

Malcolm listened and heard moans on the breeze. He smiled and slowly moved into Hans's arms. He needed to be held right then. "Give me a few minutes."

"Take your time," Hans told him, smoothing his forehead.

Malcolm took a few more minutes to catch his breath and then backed away, tugging Hans to his feet before pressing him back against the side, his long, thick cock jutting straight out. Malcolm stroked him and settled in the water, sucking Hans's cock between his greedy lips. Hans flexed his hips, and Malcolm sucked him harder, giving as much as Hans had given to him.

Hans was amazing to look at and tasty as hell, all rich musk and man. Cradling his balls, Malcolm massaged the smoothly shaved skin, teasing and sucking until Hans's legs shook enough to slosh the water. "Jesus Christ," Hans moaned shakily, and Malcolm took him deep, burying his nose in his skin, inhaling deeply. It took a few seconds for Hans's scent to come through the spice of the chlorine, but it did, and it drove Malcolm's passion.

When Hans groaned long and deep, Malcolm backed away, stroking and twisting his hand around Hans's thick length until he threw his head back, mouth hanging open. Hans came in a rush, shaking his release and gripping Malcolm's shoulder. As he came down, he released his grip and kissed Hans deeply. "I think we need to go inside," Malcolm suggested, and Hans nodded.

Malcolm got the towels and handed some to Hans. He got out of the tub and opened the sliding door, helping Hans inside. As soon as the door was closed and they'd dried each other, he pulled down the covers and climbed into bed next to Hans.

THE FOLLOWING morning, Malcolm was as stiff as he'd feared. Moving was painful and walking a chore. Skiing was out of the question, so after breakfast he sat in the lodge while Hans went out once again. Hans didn't show any outward signs, but Malcolm knew he had to be disappointed. They had come all this way to do things together, and Malcolm was laid up in a chair. He was tempted to just say to hell with it and go out, but his hip ached at the thought. So Hans had helped him to the lodge and then said good-bye with a soft kiss before striding out.

After a few hours, he returned, and they had a wonderful lunch before packing up and loading everything into the car. The return trip was quiet. Malcolm didn't feel like talking and was afraid that Hans was disappointed.

"I thought we'd stop in Madison on the way back," Hans said. "The sun is out, and we could wander South Street a little if you feel up to it."

"Sure," Malcolm answered. He had taken another pain pill, and it was working. He hoped this discomfort wouldn't last for too long and he could get back to normal. Malcolm turned and smiled. "I'm sorry things didn't work out."

Hans reached over and took his hand. "Things happen. I got to ski and had a great time on the slopes. I would have had a better time if you'd been there with me. But I understand." He squeezed his hand again. "Maybe skiing wasn't the best activity for both of us."

"I had fun."

"Next time you can decide what we do," Hans offered.

"Why don't we find something we both like? There's a lot to do in Chicago. We could go down for a day. See a show? Go shopping?" Hans didn't seem enthused about either one. "See dinosaurs?"

Hans's eyes lit up. "That sounds like fun."

"Then I'll get us tickets and make arrangements to visit the Field Museum. They have an amazing dinosaur collection. If it's nice, there are more things to do, like Millennium Park. If not, there are other things we can do."

"Awesome, let's do that, then, and maybe when the weather gets better, we can see about scuba diving. They often start in a pool so you can get used to it. We could sign you up for lessons. There's a whole different world under the water."

The idea both scared and intrigued him. "I'll give it a try."

Hans turned off the freeway and made his way through the city toward downtown. "That's what I like about you. You're willing to try new things, even after what happened this weekend."

"Well, maybe we can avoid things that go downhill really fast without a car around me." Malcolm was more than a little relieved that Hans didn't think him an uncoordinated fuddy-duddy.

"Deal," Hans said and parked the car.

It was indeed sunny, but cold. Malcolm pulled on his coat, hat, and gloves before getting out of the car. As cold as it was, South Street was teeming with people wandering past the shops. It was nice to see so many people, and Hans led the way down the sidewalk.

"There's a really nice coffee shop in the next block, and we can stop into the British bakery for a scone."

A bookstore caught Malcolm's eye, and he motioned. Hans pulled open the door, and they went inside. Used bookstores always had the same smell. He could close his eyes and know he was in one by the scent of paper, ink, and a touch of mustiness that old books always had, especially in collections.

"Look." Malcolm pointed at a shelf of Hans's titles. He walked over and picked up the one title he didn't have. He tucked it under his arm with a smile. "Will you sign this one for me if I get it?"

"Of course," Hans said with delight. Malcolm paid for the book, and they left the store and continued down the street to the bakery. "I love their ginger scones." Hans got two and some coffee.

They sat together and had their snack before moving on. The ache in Malcolm's hip increased as he sat, but he walked the next few blocks before they turned around and window-shopped the other side. Hans spent some time in a ski shop, and they both perused an antique store.

"I think I'm about to give up," Malcolm confessed, and Hans led him back to the car and began the ride home. "That was nice."

"Are you sure you're okay? Should you see a doctor?"

"I'm sure it's just a bad bruise, and it'll get better with time." It was hell getting older, but he sure wasn't going to say that. The last thing he needed was to be reminded of the difference in their ages. It was becoming clearer to him that he could never keep up with Hans, no matter how much he might want to. He was a decade younger, had more energy, and was interested in things Malcolm would never be good at. He closed his eyes once they reached the highway. Hans drove, and Malcolm nodded off after a little while.

"I feel so bad. This should have been so much more fun for you," Malcolm said when he woke from his little nap.

"It was a great weekend. Things didn't turn out as I envisioned, but that's okay. It wasn't your fault you got hurt." Hans seemed understanding, but Malcolm wondered how long that would last. Hans would eventually get tired of having to go at Malcolm's speed.

Malcolm kept quiet, and when Hans pulled up to his house, he got out of the car and waited for Hans to open the trunk.

"I'll get your bag. You go on in and put your feet up. I'll be right behind you." Hans was already getting his bag, and Malcolm slowly hobbled up to the front door and went inside. He took off his coat, draping it over the back of the nearest chair before sinking into his favorite one and slowly settling his feet on an ottoman. Hans came inside and went up the stairs. Malcolm groaned and felt like an idiot... an old, foolish one. Why in the hell would an active, virile guy like Hans want him?

"You don't have to stick around, Hans. I'm going to crawl upstairs, try to take a bath if I can get myself down into the tub, and then just go to bed." They had had a nice weekend, even with his injury, but Malcolm was quickly seeing that he'd been fooling himself.

"I put some hot water on the stove to heat, and I thought I'd make some tea." He didn't seem to have heard what Malcolm had said—or he was completely ignoring him. "I'll also make you some dinner in a few hours."

"Hans, you don't need to do that."

"Yes, I do. I took you skiing and got you hurt, so I'll help take care of you." Hans took off his coat and added it alongside Malcolm's.

"I'll be fine."

Hans crossed his arms over his chest. "Do you want me to go? Is that what you're trying to tell me? I thought we had a nice weekend, and I didn't want it to end."

He turned away, and Malcolm bit his lower lip. He did want Hans to stay but was afraid to say so. It was dangerous to want what wasn't good for him.

"A quiet dinner would be nice." Malcolm heard himself and nearly groaned. Now that they were back in his own house, the one he'd shared with David, the thought of bringing Hans up to the room and bed they'd shared was more than he could do. Dinner would have to suffice for now. The fact that they'd had sex while at the ski lodge was fine, but that wasn't the same as upstairs in his house, and even if they didn't do anything sexual because of his hip, the thought of someone other than David in their bed was too much. "I can't offer anything more than that."

"We've spent the last two days together, and I've seen as much of you as there is to see, tasted you, felt you tremble under me, and now you get shy?" There was a touch of heat in Hans's voice, tinged with disappointment.

Malcolm knew he was probably being stupid, but he wasn't ready to give up… what? He knew he wasn't giving up anything, not really. "It's just what I can do now."

"Is this one of those 'because you're older' things?" Hans asked.

"No. This is one of those 'I lost my partner of twenty years' things. I really need you to try to be patient. Certain things are hard, especially in this house." That was a partial lie. The age difference seemed to be growing as an issue in Malcolm's mind.

Hans saved him from a full explanation with a gentle nod and then left the room. He returned with mugs of tea and set one on the table beside him. Malcolm had closed his eyes and was trying to will his hip to relax, hoping some of the discomfort would subside.

It did no good, and Malcolm sipped his tea for a few minutes before leveraging himself out of the chair to limp into the kitchen. "I'll help you," Hans said, following him.

"The problem is, I don't have much in the house at the moment." Malcolm looked through his nearly bare refrigerator and an equally empty freezer and figured someone who delivered was probably their best bet for food.

"Go back in the living room and sit down. I'll run out to get something and bring it back."

Malcolm expected Hans to kiss him, but he just walked away, and Malcolm heard him getting ready and then leaving the house with the *thunk* of the front door closing.

116

Maybe this whole thing between them was a mistake. He had never been a guy who worried about his feelings. When David had entered his life, they'd been happy, and he'd understood what he was feeling and what he wanted. Most of his career, he'd gone for what he wanted. He knew he wanted Hans in his life, but he wasn't sure if that was fair to Hans. He had no doubt there were things that Hans was going to want to do and places he would want to go that he would never be able to do or keep up with. In a nutshell, he was a quiet tax attorney, and his days of extreme sports were over. Not that skiing was that kind of activity, but he hadn't even been able to do something relatively normal like that without getting hurt.

He had read Hans's books, and he had little doubt that Hans had done a lot of the things that were described. Malcolm could never keep up, and it was only a matter of time before Hans became bored with him and wanted to move on. He couldn't blame him. Hans deserved someone who could keep up with him and loved the same things he did. Not a guy who was more comfortable in an office than scuba diving.

"God," Malcolm swore, clenching his fists. If David could have heard him vacillating like this, he probably would have punched him. Hell, he wanted to hit himself. He was acting like a worried teenager after a first kiss. He needed to get it together, and he wished he could. He knew things would change, but maybe he hadn't been prepared for how much or how fast.

The house filled with the spice of Greek food as soon as Hans returned. "I thought we could have gyros." He lifted the bag before striding through the room and back toward the kitchen.

Malcolm got out of the chair once again, his hip stiff and protesting. In the kitchen, he got out knives and forks as well as plates and sat across from Hans at the table. They probably needed to talk, but Malcolm wasn't in the mood at the moment. He needed some time to think.

"I can hear the gears turning," Hans said quietly.

"What?" Malcolm asked as he tried to focus his wandering thoughts.

"In your head. You've been quiet a lot."

"I know. I'm sorry."

"You know, it's okay. A lot has happened in the past month or so. But I'll listen if you want to talk about it."

"Not yet, okay?" He felt talked out about what he couldn't do a damn thing to change.... David was gone, and no amount of talking could bring him back. Malcolm was ten years older than Hans, and nothing could change their age difference or the fact that Hans was so much more active than he was. In some ways Hans made him feel younger again, but mostly Malcolm felt old. He took a bite of his dinner and figured it was best to concentrate on the food rather than the constant swirl of indecision that seemed to rule his head at the moment.

In the end, they ate in near silence—and not the comfortable, pleasant kind where energy and possibilities kept him on his toes. This was the kind of meal where he was so damned tired he nearly fell asleep at the table. Hell, even that made him feel older. By the time they were done eating, Malcolm had worked himself into a real funk.

Hans helped clear away the dishes, and then he pulled Malcolm into his arms, which was unexpected. "I know we went a lot faster and a lot further this weekend than you planned. Sometimes things happen, and I hope this silence isn't because you're freaking out over... I don't know, starting to move on a little." Hans hugged him tight. "I'm patient, Malcolm, and I understand the need to heal."

"Thanks," Malcolm said, hiding behind Hans's explanation because he wasn't ready to offer a better one.

"I'll talk to you soon." Hans kissed him lightly and then let his arms fall to his sides before walking through the house. Malcolm followed more slowly, and once Hans had his coat on, Malcolm saw him to the door and watched as he got into his car.

Closing the door, he was even more unsettled than he'd been before Hans had left. Things felt out of sorts all around him, like his skin didn't quite fit anymore and he didn't know how to resize it. Maybe he'd feel better with some sleep.

Chapter 7

THE ENTIRE following week, it seemed like a cloud had settled around Malcolm and wouldn't go away. He did his work, but tasks required a little more concentration or focus than they usually did. Sometimes he didn't notice it, but when he was alone, that cloud got thicker, and the more he tried to puzzle it out, the more elusive and wispy the cloud became, so he just couldn't grasp what was wrong with him.

"Jane, can you make him an appointment for next week so we can put this to bed?" Malcolm asked and set a file of papers on her desk as he headed out to yet another meeting.

"Certainly," she answered and efficiently got right onto the task. "You okay?" she asked, holding the phone in her hand.

"Yes."

"You won't be," Ellen said from her desk nearby. "Gary is on his way in. He insisted on speaking with you. I told him he needed to make an appointment, but he said you'd see him if you knew what was good for you."

Malcolm had hoped to have five minutes in the conference room before his client meeting, but that had just evaporated, especially since Gary was storming his way across the office. "What do you need, Gary?" Malcolm asked. He motioned him inside what had once been Gary's office and closed the door.

"I'm going to sue all of you," he announced with bravado, "and I'm going to bring ethics charges against you with the bar association."

"Sure you are," Malcolm said as he sat in one of the chairs to get comfortable. Maybe this would be entertaining. "First off, if you really were, you'd have done it by now, so what's all the drama? You decided to leave—we didn't force you." And things were better off without his chaotic energy in the office. "So come to the point."

"You're dating one of your clients," Gary accused.

"No, I'm not. He *was* a client. Our business was concluded, and we met again separately outside the office." That his brother had been a witness was a point in his favor. "What do you want, Gary? Did you think you'd share that bit of information and then use it to try to get something?"

"I want to return to the firm," Gary said.

"So you thought you'd try to use some perceived leverage to do it?" Malcolm shook his head. "I don't think so. First, you have no basis for any sort of charges, and second, you should look at the agreement you signed when you took your buyout." Malcolm stood. "You agreed to a final settlement and stated that no issues or litigation were outstanding between you and the partners. In other words, you pretty much gave up your right to sue us." Malcolm wondered how he could have seen Gary as a friend. He was a weasel and as self-centered as they came. "So what is this visit really about? You need a job?"

"Yes," Gary answered after most of his cockiness had evaporated.

"There's not much I can do for you. The firm won't take you back." Too many people had realized how much better the office was with Gary gone, and even his one-time supporters wouldn't allow that to happen. "I suggest you start your own firm and hang out a shingle or really start looking in earnest with other firms."

"I knew you wouldn't help," Gary groused.

"There's nothing I can do." At least that attitude explained why Gary had come in all guns blazing and trying to use whatever angle he thought he could work. He checked his watch and motioned toward the door. "I have to go to a meeting, and you need to figure out what you're going to do. If there was something I could do to help, I would, but your bridges with this firm were pretty much incinerated when you left." He waited for Gary to leave his office and followed him to the elevator.

"Call me directly if he tries to return," Malcolm told the receptionist and hurried to his meeting. He had no idea why, but Malcolm had the feeling that Gary was going to show up again like some sort of bad penny. He wished he knew what his game was.

"MALCOLM," JANE said when he returned to his office an hour later. "Hans called and asked if you'd call him back."

"Thanks," Malcolm said with a half smile and went right into his office, closing the door. Inside he organized his notes and then returned Hans's call from his cell. "How is the writing going?" They hadn't talked at all that week and had exchanged just a few texts. Hans had been buried in a manuscript, and Malcolm hadn't wanted to disturb him. Apparently the ski trip had been very good for his muse.

"Great. The words have been flowing, and I think the book is going to be amazing."

Energy flowed through the phone, and Malcolm felt himself getting swept along with it. The excitement was enticing, and it sent Malcolm's mind and body racing.

"I was wondering if you wanted to get something for dinner. I've been here all week, and I'd love some company." There was something in his voice that hadn't been there before, and it sent a winter chill racing up Malcolm's spine.

"Sure," Malcolm answered before he could second-guess himself. He took a deep breath and firmed his resolve to do what he'd told himself all week had to be done. His rush of desire quickly gave way to the cold reality of what he knew he had to do. "Do you want me to make a reservation?"

"Sure," Hans said. They agreed to meet at Hans's house, and Malcolm asked Jane for a recommendation.

"I'll see what I can come up with for you," Jane said with a smile that faded quickly as she closed his office door. "All right, what act of stupidity are you about to commit?"

"I don't know what you mean," Malcolm said and returned his attention to the papers on his desk.

"Yeah, you're as innocent as the driven snow, and I'm the dominatrix from hell."

Malcolm chuckled at her imagery as she stalked closer to his desk. Jane might work for him, but when she got like this, it was best if he let her have her head. She would have made a great lawyer, and one Malcolm would not want to meet on the other side in the courtroom.

"So what's going on?"

"Why do you care so much?" Malcolm asked.

She rested her hands on his desk and leaned over it. "Because you're the best damned boss I have ever had. You don't try to look down my top or up my dress, and you treat me as an equal and a human being. You're thoughtful, and you're a good man. I care because for the last fifteen months I have watched the wonderful boss I used to laugh with go through hell and back, and just when you're starting to come out of all that quagmire, I can feel you pulling yourself back, and I don't know why. Up until this past week, you looked forward to things." She leaned closer. "Don't think I don't notice the way you hummed to yourself when you thought you were alone. You used to do that before David got sick. You were happy, and now that stopped all of a sudden. This week you've been just like you were months ago, so I figured you'd either done something really manly—read, 'stupid'—or were about to."

"I can't believe you just said all that." He swallowed. "Or that I'm so transparent."

"Only to those of us who care about you." She sat down, and her posture softened. "Now what's the deal? And be careful how you answer, because stupidity is going to cost you even more flowers." She raised her eyebrows. "Lots of them."

"I have an appointment in five minutes."

"I moved it back until eleven thirty and told Ellen that we were having a private conversation and to hold your calls. Now talk to me. I'm not just your assistant, I'm your friend."

"I like Hans," Malcolm said, giving in and opening up.

"And you're afraid of what David would think?" Jane asked, but Malcolm shook his head. "Good. Because he'd want you to move on. You know that."

"He would. But I still can't get my head around having someone who isn't David in my life like that. But I will. It's slow, but I can feel that I want to open up. That sounds stupid even to me, but I think you get it."

"Is Hans pushing you?" Jane asked.

"No."

"Then what's the problem? Is it his age?" She'd hit the bull's-eye. "That's just a number, and it doesn't affect who we love."

"But he'll get bored with me." Malcolm let his fear slip out. "I can't keep up with him." He sighed like some lovesick teenager. "You didn't see him on those slopes. He looked like he owned them, and he was so graceful and…." Malcolm clamped his eyes shut, and he could see Hans on that slope. "He goes diving and he jumps out of planes, for God's sake. I went down a ski slope and got laid up sore for a week. I can't keep up with him, and I never will be able to." He shook his head because he was not going to let his eyes water.

"Malcolm, I…."

"There's nothing you or anyone can do. If I could, I'd love to be ten years younger, but then I'd have David and almost everything I could want in the world." He missed him so very much every single day. Everyone had said that time would heal his loss, but Malcolm wasn't so sure about that. "I still miss him each and every day."

Jane scoffed. "Of course you do, and you will for the rest of your life. But that doesn't mean you can't love again. I think that's what's happening, and it scares you."

"No, it doesn't," Malcolm said weakly and way too fast.

Jane cocked her eyebrow and stared at him.

"I'm not in love with Hans."

"I didn't say you were, but maybe you could be, and that's what has you wetting yourself. You may not think you're ready and all that—maybe you aren't—but you shouldn't do something stupid to ensure that you never find out."

"What is this stupid thing you keep referring to?" Malcolm challenged.

"I don't know. Like not calling him all week and then making some boneheaded decision that it would be better for him if you walked away… or some such crap."

Damn it, how did Jane know what he was thinking? He really needed to learn to school his expression better. "I don't know what I'm going to do."

"Then try letting things work out on their own and see what happens. You deserve the chance to be happy, despite your own best efforts." Jane rolled her eyes. "Now I believe you have that meeting you were so worried about."

Malcolm stood and gathered his materials. "You'd think you were the senior partner."

"Please, like I'd ever want your job." She flashed him a grin. "Although I could use a raise."

She pulled open the door and left his office. Malcolm wondered what the heck he'd done to deserve her and then left for his meeting. Thankfully it seemed that Jane had taken pity on him, and when she rescheduled the meeting, she'd arranged for food, so he wouldn't have to go without lunch. The more he thought about it, maybe Jane was right. With all she did for him, maybe she did deserve a raise. Jane poked her head back in the doorway.

"Oh, and flowers would be nice."

She flashed him another smile. Malcolm groaned and reconsidered the raise.

BY THE time he was to meet Hans at his home, Malcolm was completely at a loss for what he should do. In the end he decided that Jane was probably right and he should see where things went between them. As soon as he made that decision, the blue mood and the fog lifted, and he realized the whole week he'd made himself miserable for nothing.

"I hope you're in the mood for Italian," Malcolm said when Hans answered the door. He expected Hans's usual smile and energy, but instead Hans appeared worried and bit his lower lip. Malcolm immediately began to wonder if he hadn't been invited over because Hans had come to his senses and realized Malcolm wasn't for him.

"Please come in," Hans said, but he didn't make any move to kiss or even approach his personal space.

"What's going on?" Malcolm asked and checked his watch. "I made a reservation because I thought you wanted to go to dinner, but maybe I should call to cancel it." He felt gravity squeezing in on all sides.

Hans nodded and offered to take Malcolm's coat. He hung it up and led Malcolm into the bright living room. "Would you like a drink?"

Malcolm noticed the bottles that sat on one of the side tables and wondered just how much Hans had been drinking.

"I'm fine." Malcolm wanted to know what was going on. He pulled out his phone, canceled the dinner reservations, and then shoved the phone back into his pocket. "Do you want to tell me what's going on, or am I supposed to guess?"

Hans motioned to the chair, and Malcolm sat down, while Hans did the same on the sofa. Malcolm was beginning to get the idea that he needn't have worried all week about what he was going to do about Hans because this was the end of whatever they'd had between them. Malcolm knew he was jumping to a conclusion, but it seemed like a good one.

"I'm not sure how to say this."

"Okay, I can make it easy on you. I understand that you don't want to date someone as old as I am, and that you don't think I'll be able to keep up with you, and that someday you'll probably get bored with me, so you figure you'll walk away now before we both get hurt." He began to get up.

"No," Hans said rather frantically. "I wasn't breaking up with you, though it seems you have a pretty long list of fears." Hans stood and came closer. "I think we need to talk about what you just said, but I...." Hans paused and sighed. "This is going to freak you out, and I don't want you to, but I know I have to tell you. I went to the doctor on Tuesday. It was a routine appointment for a physical, and they found something. We're not sure what it is, but they did a CAT scan and there's a spot on my lung." Hans looked scared half to death.

Deep winter cold shot up Malcolm's spine, fanning out in tendrils that froze through his veins and threatened to choke off his ability to breathe. Malcolm didn't remember standing up, but he was halfway across the room to the door before he realized where he was, and he wasn't sure what he was doing. "Have they done a biopsy?" Malcolm asked, his mouth and tongue bone dry. He'd asked that question before. He'd had this kind of conversation before. It hadn't ended well at all: months of chemotherapy and watching David get thinner and thinner, more and more frail until he could barely hold his head up or say a word. He couldn't go through that again.

"They're doing it on Monday. The plan is for them to do surgery, see what's actually there, remove the spot, and biopsy it."

His hand shook, and Malcolm slowly walked back toward him and sat down in what felt like slow motion.

"After that they'll know what course of treatment I'm going to need."

Malcolm was silent. Words escaped him. This hadn't been anywhere on his radar. Hans was young, too young, for all this. Hell, David had been too young as well. "Did they give you any idea what they think it is?"

"No. They don't know, and I've been burying myself in my work so I don't think about it too much."

Hans turned toward him, and Malcolm wondered what he could say. He was at a complete loss, and the cold wasn't going away. It had him firmly in the clutches of an emotional ice age that didn't appear to be willing to thaw anytime soon.

"I wasn't going to tell you until I knew something for sure, but I don't know how much more not knowing I can handle." Hans sighed, and Malcolm scooted closer, put his arms around him, and pulled him close.

Malcolm made some foreign sound deep in his throat. Words were impossible as the lump built to grapefruit size. The déjà vu was nearly overwhelming, and yet he knew he had to be strong and couldn't let his fear overtake him.

"I know," he managed to say.

"I didn't want you to have to go through this again. You don't deserve that, and I was hoping this whole thing would turn out to be nothing, and then we could... I don't know." Hans lifted his gaze. "I know you're scared, and from what you said earlier, you have quite a laundry list of issues, and this is only adding to them."

"I don't know why I let my fear get the better of me." The things he'd been afraid of before now seemed so stupid. He'd let his imagination run away with him because he thought Hans might get tired of him. Now the same monster that had taken David might take Hans as well. That was worth being afraid of.

"Did I do something to make you feel that way?" Hans asked, and it took Malcolm a second to realize he was referring to his earlier outburst.

"I am older than you, and it seems there's no way I can keep up with you. I don't dive or jump out of airplanes...."

"I don't jump out of airplanes. I'm afraid of heights."

"But you go up hills to ski."

"That doesn't seem like heights to me, and I've gotten used to it, I guess. The thing is, there's no way I'm going to jump out of a plane, and I'm not going to get tired of you because you don't want to ski or dive."

"But...."

"Just get over yourself," Hans teased. "There are a lot more important things, like the fact that we have fun together and that we're both willing to try new things. Stagnation is death, and I refuse to be still, but that doesn't mean I'm going to leave you behind."

Malcolm couldn't believe they were talking about this now. Hans had just told him he might have cancer, and now he was talking about Malcolm's insecurities.

"And just for the record, how could I get bored with you?" Hans pulled away and glared at him. "You're funny and you're caring. Maybe you're a little buttoned-up sometimes, but that's not boring, just stuffy. I can deal with stuffy as long as you let me pull you out of your shell sometimes."

Malcolm was really having a tough time understanding how Hans could just let all this go. "What about sex?" Malcolm asked. "I'm older, and you're going to want more than I can give you. What if I'm too tired, and you…?" He couldn't say it.

"I don't cheat, and you know it. I've been on the receiving end of that, and I'd never do that to anyone. And in case you haven't guessed, I'm not some teenager who's just one huge set of raging hormones. So you're a little older than me. Big deal." Hans twirled his finger in the air. "Sometimes you make the biggest deal of the littlest things, and for the record, all you have to do is tell me if something is bothering you. Holding everything inside isn't good. We aren't stupid kids. We can talk to one another."

"Fine." Hans said that the difference in their ages didn't matter, but words were one thing, actions another. While Malcolm felt a little better about where things stood between them, there was still the fact that Hans might have cancer. How in the hell could he tell Hans that he couldn't go through all that again?

"I know what's going through your head," Hans said after a while. They'd been sitting quietly, and Malcolm had been wondering what he was going to do.

"You do?"

"Sure. And I don't blame you. After David and everything you did to take care of him, you can't go through all that again. Why do you think I didn't tell you right away?"

"You expected me to walk away," Malcolm said.

Hans nodded once. "I still do. This is a lot for me to take on, but I know after what you went through with David, I can't expect you to willingly go through that again." Hans reached across the small space that separated them on the sofa and stroked his cheek. "You're…."

"I'm just a man, the same as you." Malcolm wasn't sure what he was going to do, but Hans thinking he'd leave made him angry, and he could feel his heels digging in. Maybe that was what Hans had wanted and hoped for. Malcolm wasn't sure, but in a few seconds, without giving it much thought, because he knew if he did, he'd run for the hills, Malcolm shifted closer and held Hans tighter. "And I'm here and I'll stay here."

That felt right, and some of the cold that had gripped him began to melt. He was still scared as hell. He'd finally been willing to open up, and his old enemy, the disease that had taken David from him, had returned and was trying to claim someone else.

"Are you sure? I won't blame you if this is too much." Hans had to be on the edge of an emotional abyss. Malcolm remembered how David had been blindsided and scared out of his wits at this point. The not knowing was always bad, and he and David had ridden a roller coaster of good and bad news for months. Malcolm hoped like hell he didn't have to go through all that again, but at the moment, he needed to put his fear and worry aside to help Hans.

"You need to keep calm and try not to worry. I know it's hard, but until you know for sure, your own imagination is your worst enemy." He remembered how David had nearly shut down at this point. "There isn't anything either of us can do right now, so it's best to try to go on with normal things." Malcolm heard his own words, but ever since David's diagnosis, his life had been anything but normal. Still, he knew what he was saying was correct. He just wasn't sure if he was saying it to reassure Hans or himself. Maybe both of them, if he were honest.

"How do you suggest doing that?"

"That's one question I wish I could answer. David and I worried for days when he was first diagnosed. There were biopsies, treatment plans, and everyone was so optimistic. But this disease has a mind of its own, and sometimes it does what it wants."

"That's so very reassuring," Hans said.

"I'm sorry. It's hard for me to be positive about this. But I will be there, and I'll do what I can to help you." He knew he was putting some distance between them, and he didn't mean to, but he couldn't help it.

"Is that all you'll do?" Hans asked.

Malcolm closed his eyes, clamping them tightly. "I don't know if I can do anything more. I did that once before, and look how it turned out."

"David died because of his disease. It didn't have anything to do with you. It wasn't your bad luck or something."

"No, it wasn't. But it was still hell," Malcolm said. He opened his eyes when images came to him of David in bed, unable to move because he didn't have the energy, and Malcolm taking care of him day and night, nurses living with them, and Malcolm feeling guilty every time he left for work because he was afraid that something might happen to David while he was away.

"Knowing how things turned out, would you change anything? Would you still date and fall in love with him?" Hans asked.

Without hesitation Malcolm nodded. "Yes. I'd do it all again. The time we had together was so amazing. I'd walk through hell and back for him again and again."

Hans sighed. "That's all I want. Someone willing to do that for me." Hans stood and shuffled to the other side of the room. "I thought I'd found someone, but you know how that turned out. And then I met you. Yes, I learned that it may have been too soon, and that we'd have to take things slowly, but I saw you in that restaurant with your brother and my pulse raced and my heart pounded in my ears. I saw passion and kindness in your eyes, and I thought you were hot."

"Me? Hot?"

"Yes. You're hot, and you're also one hell of a man," Hans said, poking the air with his finger. "But I guess everyone has their limits, and I just found yours." He stalked closer. "Malcolm, I understand that you can't go through this all over again. I really do." Hans poured a shot of bourbon and downed it in a single gulp. "As usual, my timing really sucks. But I suppose it's better that something like this happened now rather than later. Like you said earlier, we can go our separate ways without it hurting too damn bad." He poured another hit of the liquor and drank it.

"You're getting drunk," Malcolm said as gently as he could.

"Doesn't matter. At least if I'm drunk I can forget for a few hours that I might have cancer." He began rocking a little from side to side.

Malcolm hurried over to Hans and guided him down into one of the chairs. Then he took the glass and went into the kitchen for a glass of water. He handed it to Hans and encouraged him to drink it.

"I should have known this was too much for you, but I really hoped, you know…?" Hans held the glass in both hands like it would keep him above water. "I fell in love with you," Hans said. "I didn't want to. I knew you were still mourning David, but I did anyway. And I was a fool." He drank the rest of the water.

Malcolm wanted to tell Hans that he wasn't a fool, that he hadn't been the only one going down that road, but he stopped himself cold. He could not let this happen again. He would be there to help Hans as much as he could, because no one should have to go through something like this alone, but he couldn't get close again. That was more than he could handle.

"You need to ease off on the drinking and get some food," Malcolm said as he left to see what was in the kitchen. He found some fixings and made some sandwiches, then brought one in to Hans. He put the plate into his hands and sat next to him. "Eat."

Hans picked up the ham sandwich and took a bite. His movements were automatic, and Malcolm doubted he tasted anything. He wasn't particularly hungry either, but Malcolm ate and worried. Hans was not normally a quiet man. He talked and was open and fun.

"How is the book coming?" Malcolm asked.

Hans turned away from where he'd been staring at the wall. "It's crap. I worked on it all week, and I'm probably going to have to rewrite everything I did because of all this." Of course, he was a bad judge of his own work, and only a little distance would tell for sure.

Hans set his plate on the table without looking at it. When he turned to Malcolm, his eyes were flat. Talking about his work and his stories always got Hans excited. He'd light up and forget about almost everything else. Malcolm had to do something. He understood the worry and fear.

"Damn it," Malcolm said under his breath. He stood and grabbed the plates, then took them back into the kitchen. He tossed the sandwiches into the trash and then rinsed out all the glasses. He even capped the liquor before opening the closet door and getting Hans's coat. "Come on."

"What? I want to stay here."

"Put on the coat. We're getting out of here. There's nothing you can do until Monday, so worrying and fixating on it won't make a damn bit of difference." He got his own coat, and once Hans was dressed for the cold, he led him out to his car.

"Where are we going?"

"First thing, we're going to have some dinner. I know a nice place with the best cake." He headed toward the freeway.

"The same Mexican place?" Hans asked. "I'm really not in the mood to be around people."

"We need to eat, and sitting at home is the wrong thing to do. You're going to have to trust me on this." He made the turn onto Capitol Drive and continued, catching the lights. "There is nothing scarier than where you are right now. David kept saying that all he wanted was to know. He could deal with anything once he had an answer. Maybe he was right and maybe not, but you have to be feeling the same way."

"I don't know what to feel. I could have cancer, and the person I thought might care for me, doesn't. Well, not enough." Hans stared straight ahead, and Malcolm simply drove. They reached the highway, and Malcolm merged onto it, heading toward and then through downtown.

Hans was wrong—Malcolm did care. In fact, Hans's words were like a knife to his gut because he truly did care and was falling in love with him. But going through cancer with another loved one was more than he thought he could take. He hated that disease, and it kept taking a toll on his life. Malcolm felt his eyes fill, and then the moisture overflowed, running down his cheeks. He couldn't stop it and was finding it hard to drive. But he didn't dare wipe his eyes because he didn't want Hans to see him like this.

Malcolm dared a glance at Hans, and his chest clenched at the way he sat, hunched on the seat, a finger between his lips, probably biting his nails. Malcolm touched his arm, and Hans lowered his hand to the armrest between them. Malcolm held it, entwining their fingers. He didn't want Hans to feel alone.

Once they reached the restaurant, they found it busy, but they were able to get a table in the bar. "What would you like?" Malcolm asked.

"I'm not hungry," Hans whispered just loudly enough that Malcolm could hear him over the din. Malcolm opened the menu and ordered what he remembered Hans had had the last time and then got something for himself.

"You have to eat." Malcolm knew some of Hans's mood was his fault, and he wanted to dispel it, but his own fear stood right in the way like a twelve-foot stone garden wall. "So Monday you go in for surgery. Did they leave any specific instructions for preparation?"

"I can't eat after 6:00 p.m. on Sunday, and I'm to be at the hospital at 6:00 a.m."

"All right." Malcolm excused himself to go to the bathroom and stepped around the corner. He pulled his phone out of his pocket.

"Malcolm," Jane said when she answered the call. "What exploded?"

Malcolm wished he'd given a little more thought to what he was going to say. "I need to be out of the office on Monday. Please clear my day as best you can."

"Just a minute," Jane said, and Malcolm waited. "Okay. I'm somewhere quiet. I'll check your schedule in the morning and can easily clear any internal meetings. Then I'll start contacting clients to reschedule." She was clearly waiting for an explanation. "Should I contact you on your cell?"

"You can try. But cell service will be spotty at best."

"Why, are you going into the hospital?"

Damn, nothing got by her. He should have known.

"I'll be sitting with a friend." That was all he could tell her. Hans's health issue was not his to talk about. "I'll call you when I can."

"All right. I hope your friend comes through well and everything is all right."

"Me too," Malcolm said. He ended the call and put his phone back in his pocket before using the bathroom and then returning to the table. "I called Jane and had her clear my schedule on Monday. I'll take you to the hospital and sit with you while you're there."

"You don't have to do that. I can manage to get myself there. They said they'd probably keep me overnight and then send me home. It shouldn't be that big of a deal." Hans was making light of it, but the darkness in his eyes spoke of his worry.

Malcolm didn't argue. It wouldn't do any good at the moment. He intended to take Hans in and stay with him, and that was that. He'd been through this before—he knew what to expect—and he wasn't going to let Hans do it alone.

"You run hot and cold sometimes," Hans said after a few minutes. "You say you're going to be there, and yet I can feel you pulling away from me. You cleared your schedule on Monday so you could be with me at the hospital, and yet you don't know if you can go through this again. I don't understand."

"Neither do I," Malcolm said. "You're just going to have to give me a little time too. Your news has thrown me back into everything I went through with David."

"But you said you'd do it all over again."

"Yeah, I did, and I would." It was strange the way that simple statement pulled him in two directions. The real question was, would he do it all over again, but with Hans? With David, the love of his life, yes, he'd do it again. He'd go through hell so they could have the nearly twenty amazing years they'd had together. And yes, he'd give anything to have those twenty years back, even knowing how they ended. But with Hans there was so little history and…. He was being a dick. The unsaid question was written all over Hans's face, and Malcolm wished like hell he had an answer for him.

The server brought their food, and it drew Hans's attention away from him. This whole situation was almost overwhelming, and Malcolm needed a little time to think, but he doubted he was going to get it. Hans needed someone, that Malcolm knew without a doubt, and Hans had come to him. Malcolm knew he wouldn't turn his back on him. But all that kept running through his head were the months of chemotherapy and treatment, the way David had slowly wasted away. The crying in the middle of the night from the pain. That was what he was afraid of. All of that had ripped Malcolm's heart out and left him feeling completely useless. He'd been unable to do anything to ease those moments of suffering when that was the one thing he wanted most in the entire world.

"Talk to me," Hans said quietly.

"I was so helpless," Malcolm said. "That was the worst part—knowing David was in pain and being able to do nothing." This was not a good time to talk about all that. "I know I wasn't the one who was ill, but I nursed him and was there for him. He had cancer, but we both went through the disease. Can you understand? It was like we both had it."

"I think I can," Hans said. "And you aren't sure you can have cancer again like that."

"I'm afraid." Malcolm took a bite of his enchilada and set down his fork. The food tasted bland even though he knew there was plenty of spice. "It's that simple. What if I fall for you and you end up the same way as David? I don't know if I can live through that again." He was trying to be as honest as he could.

"So what happens? You see me through this biopsy, and if I have cancer, then you walk away? And if I don't, we can maybe have a relationship?"

"No. I'm saying I don't know." It sounded lame to his ears. "I don't want you to go through this process alone, and I hope more than anything that this is just a scare. I care about you. I didn't expect to, and I wasn't looking for it, but you got through. Somehow you got through the grief and the resistance I tried to put up. I don't want to lose you like I did David." There, his cards were on the table as much as he could lay them out.

"Okay," Hans said and reached across the table. "You aren't going to."

"How do you know?" Malcolm pressed. "You can't. No one does."

"If I have it, then I'll fight with everything I have. You have to know that."

"Of course you will." Malcolm squeezed Hans's hand in return. "You're going to be strong and get through whatever happens. I know that." And he did. He had to. There was no way cancer was going to take someone else from his life. Malcolm could feel his resolve growing inside him. This fucking disease had stolen David away from him. He was not going to let it take Hans too. No fucking way in hell. "And I'll be there somehow." He had to be strong for Hans, and nothing else mattered.

He returned to his dinner and managed to eat most of it. Hans ate some of his as well. When they were finished, he got two pieces of cake to go and took Hans back to his house. Inside, he placed the cake in the kitchen and turned out the lights and then led Hans upstairs. He wasn't going to leave him alone, and that meant making sure Hans knew he was cared for.

"Why are we here?" Hans asked when Malcolm opened the door to his bedroom.

Malcolm looked inside the room and realized what he was doing. For the first time, he'd brought Hans to his bed, the one he'd shared with David. Up until that moment, he hadn't given it a thought, but now that he was in the room, his memories washed over him in waves. But not the guilt he'd expected. He and David had shared their lives in this room, the best and the worst. It had been theirs, but it was only a room, and the bed just a piece of furniture.

"You all right?" Hans asked. "I know this is hard for you."

"No. It's okay." He held Hans's hand and brought him into the room. The loss and pain he'd expected to feel at this moment didn't materialize. David was still here with him, but what he felt was the good memories, the happy ones. Somehow, in the past few weeks, the sadness and loss hadn't gone away, but they'd become less important and immediate. "This was where David and I spent twenty years together. We loved a lot, fought sometimes, but never went to bed angry. That was the rule we both lived by."

"I like that."

"Me too. More than once David used that to his advantage, knowing I couldn't stay angry with him for very long. I nursed and took care of David in this room." Malcolm turned to Hans. "I never thought I would be able to bring another man here. I honestly thought that part of my life was over, and then my pushy brother intervened, and I got to know you."

"You don't have to."

"It's just a room, and the bed is just a bed. I lost track of the fact that David is in my heart. He isn't here any longer." Malcolm walked to the bed and sat down. "I haven't slept on this side of the bed since I lost David. I stayed on my own side. I did all kinds of things like that to keep from acknowledging that David was gone. I knew he was gone, but I kept trying to hold on to him." Malcolm tugged Hans closer. "And as much as it scares me, you're the one who allowed me to let him go."

"But what about all this next week?"

Malcolm took a deep breath. "All I can do—we can do—is to remember to take each day as it comes. David's counselor told both of us that more than once, but I forgot it until just now. Neither of us can predict the future, and worrying about it only makes things worse. David had cancer, and as much as I'd like to change that, I can't. The one thing I don't regret is that he and I made the most of the time we had together. So I'll make you the same promise. If the news isn't good, we'll make the most of what we have." This had to be the hardest thing Malcolm had ever said. His throat ached, but he knew the words were important.

"God, I hope it doesn't come to that," Hans said. "I plan to be around for a very long time, no matter what."

Malcolm nodded, ashamed. He'd almost instantly jumped to the conclusion that Hans's news was going to be bad, and if it was, that everything would happen the way it had with David. None of that was necessarily true. "I hope so too." He had to be positive and not let what had happened to him and David color his thoughts about Hans. It was so hard, and he'd been doing it almost from the moment Hans had told him. "I'm sorry."

"We're both afraid of the same thing, but from a different perspective," Hans said, and Malcolm held him tighter. That was so true. Malcolm was scared to death because he'd already been down this road, and Hans was scared of the unknown and what might yet be.

"I hate fear," Malcolm said quietly. "Whenever I let it take over my life, everything falls apart." He knew that was what he'd done earlier. Hell, he'd been letting fear affect his decision-making as far as Hans was concerned for a while. That was what Jane had been trying to tell him earlier and what he saw when he looked back at his reaction. Twice fear had threatened to push Hans away, but there wasn't going to be a third time. "Somehow, no matter what happens, we'll figure out a way through this."

"Are you sure?" Hans asked.

"If I said yes, it would be a lie. I'm not sure of anything other than that I'm falling in love with you. I never expected to do that again, and yet here you are. I was lucky enough to have had David in my life, and I'm lucky to have you as well." For however long that might be. Malcolm had often wondered if there was a price to pay for happiness. He and David had been truly happy, so maybe his cancer was the price the universe exacted for that. Malcolm hated to think that way, but he couldn't help wondering about it.

He tugged Hans closer and down, kissing him hard, pulling the larger man down on top of him. He held Hans tightly, letting their warmth mingle. He didn't think sex was a particularly good idea on a night like this. But he knew from experience that sometimes comfort and care were more important than sex, and this felt very much like one of those times.

They undressed each other slowly and then climbed under the blankets. Malcolm pressed against Hans's broad back and held him close.

"It'll be all right, no matter what happens," Malcolm whispered into the darkness, but he didn't close his eyes or go to sleep until the small hours of the morning.

Chapter 8

THE REST of the weekend held a strong sense of déjà vu for Malcolm. He stayed with Hans and tried to keep his mind off the impending surgery, which went fairly well. The hardest thing was to keep his mind from slipping back to when he'd been in this situation for David. Every time that happened, the whole ordeal came to mind, and Malcolm had to push all of that away. On the whole he was fairly successful. He got Hans up early on Monday and to the hospital on time, where he was prepped for surgery while Malcolm waited in one of those rooms seemingly designed to add even more anxiety to the process.

"Hi, Jane," he said when his phone rang half an hour after Hans had been wheeled away.

"How is Hans?" she asked.

"In surgery now." He groaned. "I never told you I was here for him."

"You did now," she said gleefully. "What happened?"

"He's just having some tests done," Malcolm explained.

"That's the exact same thing you said about David. Is he having those kind of tests done?" Jane asked, and when Malcolm didn't answer, she filled in her own. "Malcolm, it'll be all right. These tests turn out benign all the time. You know that."

He looked around and made sure no one was sitting too close to him. "What if it isn't? I was with him all weekend, and it was like trying not to go back in time. I tried to be upbeat and say the right things most of the time, but this is ripping me apart, and I can't seem to stop it. He actually asked me if our relationship depended on the results of this test, and I couldn't say it didn't."

"If it does, I'd have to kill you," she teased, but with a note of seriousness.

"Yeah. But I kind of feel that maybe…." He stopped himself from finishing the thought.

"Look, Malcolm. What doesn't kill us makes us stronger, and you took care of David without a single complaint for all those months. You adored him, and he thought the sun rose and set around you." Jane paused, and the line went quiet. "I'm in your office. Now listen to me. You were one of those rare people who got someone who loved you with his whole heart and soul. You and David were amazing together. And then you lost him. I know that nearly killed you, but it didn't, and guess what…. You met Hans and you started living again."

"I know, Jane—" He couldn't say anything more because she cut him off.

"It comes down to one question. Do you love him? Forget about the age difference and all the other things you might be afraid of. All you have to ask yourself is how he makes you feel and what would happen if that man walked out of your life."

"I asked myself the same thing a hundred times this weekend."

"And what did you do?"

"I held Hans tighter and prayed that he'd be okay." Malcolm could feel the resolve that had carried him through the days crumbling right then. His hand shook, and he blinked as tears filled his eyes. "It's too early to say something like 'I don't know what I'd do without him.' But I want to find out how to have him and make him happy more than anything else in the world right now. This morning, before we left, I realized that the only picture I have of Hans is on my phone, and if anything happened to him, I'd have very little of him. He'd be like a ghost who came into my life and then left again without leaving a trace, and I don't want that."

"There you go. You have your answer."

Malcolm heard a squeak from behind her.

"Are you sitting in my chair?" Malcolm asked.

"Yes. It's way more comfortable than mine."

"Then why didn't you get yourself a new one like I said? Better yet, put a note on my calendar for me to talk to the partners about some of the office furniture. We need to do some proper upgrades for everyone."

"I will. And your schedule has been cleared. Now take care of Hans, and I'll see you when you come in tomorrow."

"Thanks," Malcolm said and hung up the phone. He set it on his lap and stared out at the others waiting with him. After a while a couple sat near him, talking quietly. The husband was soothing his wife, who clung to a well-used teddy bear. The man did his best to keep her calm. Malcolm looked away so he didn't intrude and decided that some coffee might be good. He went in search of some and found the cafeteria. He got three cups in a paper holder and offered the extra two cups to the young couple.

"Thank you," the man said softly. "Our son is having heart surgery."

Malcolm nodded. "I hope everything works out. How long will it be?"

"They don't know," he answered, and the woman nodded, her eyes puffy. "Why are you here?"

"My boyfriend is having a biopsy, and I have my fingers crossed," Malcolm said and returned to his seat. He found a magazine and tried to read it but had no luck. He'd brought some work, intending to try to read through it, but that wasn't going to happen either. So he ended up sitting back in the chair and willing the clock to move faster so he could get some answers.

After another hour, he had to get up and move. His mind wouldn't let him focus on anything. Now that his head was on straight and he could see things clearly, all he wanted was to be able to hold Hans's hand again. Finally the woman in charge of the waiting area came over and told him Hans was out of surgery and in recovery. "You can see him in a few minutes."

"Thank you." Malcolm sat down and waited until he was told where Hans was. He was about to leave when a man dressed in white came out to talk to the young couple.

"The surgeon asked me to come out to tell you that it's better than anyone thought. The damage to the heart was much less than predicted, and Mikey should be out of surgery soon. There is every indication that he should be fine once he recovers."

Malcolm smiled as the couple hugged each other and the woman cried on her husband's shoulder. He turned away to give them their privacy and followed the directions of the attendant to where Hans was. Malcolm entered the small room in recovery and approached Hans's bed. He was surprised when he parted the curtain to find a man sitting next to the bed, holding Hans's hand.

"It's going to be all right. I shouldn't have done what I did, and it's all my fault."

"Hans," Malcolm said softly as he entered. He wanted to shove the other guy away. Why in the hell was he holding his boyfriend's hand? Hans hadn't said anything about a brother.

"Who are you?" the man asked.

"Malcolm, Hans's boyfriend," Malcolm answered, and that had the effect he was hoping for. The man placed Hans's hand back on the bed.

"Troy," he said in a clipped tone.

Malcolm nodded. "The cheating ex. He told me about you." Malcolm was all about winning, and he was definitely going to stake his claim and make sure this Troy guy knew where things stood.

"Malcolm," Hans whispered.

Malcolm stepped closer, standing next to the bed in front of Troy. "I'm here. How do you feel? Are you in pain?" Malcolm took Hans's hand, stroking his fingers and ignoring the other man in the room.

"No. I'm good for now. Thirsty," Hans whispered, and Malcolm found a glass of ice chips on the tray and placed one between Hans's lips.

"It's going to hurt to swallow at first, so be careful." He continued stroking Hans's large hand. "Have they said how things went?"

A nurse came in to check on him. "You're doing great, Mr. Erickson. They're going to move you to a room in a few minutes. Keep sucking on those ice chips. They'll soothe your throat. The doctor said he'll be in to talk to you this afternoon." She checked Hans's monitors and asked him about pain. When Hans said it was getting worse, she injected something into his IV, and Hans closed his eyes a few minutes later.

"So Hans is seeing some old guy," Troy said once the nurse had left.

Malcolm turned around to look at Troy. He was handsome enough, with nice eyes and a strong face, but the sneer on his lips ruined the effect. "You hurt him," Malcolm said. "You pulled a life he thought he had right out from under him. Now you're back and you realize how stupid you were, and you're hoping he'll take you back. But I don't think so."

"Why, because some geezer with gray hair is the competition?" Troy smiled mockingly.

"No. Because he found love again and has moved on. It's been a long time, and you're just a footnote in his life now." Malcolm continued stroking Hans's hand. "It was nice of you to come, but Hans doesn't need you now."

"Troy," Hans whispered.

The guy smirked as he stood and leaned over the bed. "I'm here, baby," he whispered.

"This is Malcolm, my boyfriend," Hans said, his eyes only half-open. "I love him. He's good to me." Hans squeezed his hand, and just like that, the last of Malcolm's reservations lifted away. Whatever happened, he'd be there for Hans as best he could.

"I love you too, sweetheart," Malcolm said as he leaned over the bed.

"Maybe I should go," Troy said. "Unless you want me to stay with you."

"Thanks for coming, Troy. Malcolm will make sure I'm okay."

Hans closed his eyes again, and Malcolm didn't give him a triumphant grin, though he wanted to. Instead he watched as Troy gathered his coat and left the room.

"Don't you have to work?" Hans asked once Troy was gone.

"I had Jane clear my schedule so I could be here with you, remember?" Malcolm placed Hans's hand back under the bedding so he didn't get cold. "Don't worry about anything right now. Just close your eyes and go to sleep. I'll be here when you wake up again."

Hans did as Malcolm asked, and Malcolm sat down in the chair, waiting for what was going to happen next.

Eventually they moved Hans to a room, and Malcolm settled into the chair next to his bed. Hans slept on and off for hours. They talked a little, but Hans was pretty out of it. Malcolm knew it would take time for the test results to come back, and he hoped like hell everything was okay. They brought Hans a tray of food, and he ate a little of it before falling back to sleep. Malcolm used that as a chance to get some food for himself and then returned to the room.

Hans was partially awake. "Was Troy here?"

"Yes. He was with you in recovery." Malcolm wondered how he'd known about Hans's surgery unless Hans had called him.

"That was nice," Hans sighed. "I'm over him, you know. Troy probably came out of some sense of loyalty."

"Then you didn't hear him." Malcolm swallowed. "He said he was sorry, and that he was a fool and wanted you back. He seemed really sincere. I take it you don't remember any of that."

"No. He said he was sorry and wanted me back? That's nice." Hans rolled his head on the pillow. "I don't want him back. Troy is a cheater, and if he did that once, he'll do it again."

"I know." There were so many things Malcolm wanted to tell Hans, but that would all have to wait.

"I really loved him and was with him a long time." Hans sighed and closed his eyes once again. "But I'm over him."

"Did you tell him what was happening?" Malcolm asked.

"Yeah. He and I are supposed to be friends. I didn't know he'd actually come to see me." Hans yawned and closed his eyes for another nap.

MALCOLM SAT with Hans for the rest of the afternoon and into the evening. The doctor came in before dinner and pulled the curtain so he could check on Hans's bandages.

"Everything went very well, and we've sent the tissue to the lab, but I'm optimistic that it was only a small tissue growth and nothing more." He smiled. "You should heal up quickly and be able to get around easily in a few days. We were careful to go in with as small an incision as possible and disturb as little as necessary. You will be sore for a few days, but that should begin to fade."

"So I'm fine?" Hans asked.

"Yes. We need to be sure, and the test results will take a few days, but I believe this was simply a false alarm." He moved closer to the bed. "I'll be in again to see you tomorrow before we send you home. You're going to need someone to help take care of you for a few days. Getting around may be a little uncomfortable, but after that you can return to life as normal."

"Thank you, Doctor," Hans said and smiled as he turned to Malcolm.

"That's great," Malcolm told him as the old insecurities rose once again. He had to get over this. His age didn't seem to matter to Hans, so why should it matter to him? After all, Hans had chosen him over Troy. "Why don't you get some more rest? I'll be back later tonight to see you."

"Okay." Hans took his hand. "You don't know what it means to me to have you here."

Malcolm leaned over the bed, kissing Hans gently, and then he got his things and left the room. He strode through the hospital corridors and out to his car. He drove to his office, parked, and went inside, going right to his office and closing the door. Jane looked surprised as he passed, but she thankfully said nothing. Malcolm figured with his schedule clear he could have a few hours to help stay current with his work.

"Why are you still here?" he asked Jane as she came into his office.

"I had things to catch up on, and I had to watch out for you. How did it go?" Jane asked. She'd actually been able to stay out for a whole five minutes before her curiosity got the better of her.

"They think he's going to be fine and that it wasn't cancer. We need to wait for the tests to be sure, but it seems to be good news."

"Then why are you holed up in here rather than up there sitting with him?" Jane put her hands on her hips, glaring at him like she would a misbehaving child.

"Jesus, Jane, you're getting bossy," he said without looking up from his work. "I needed a few hours to get caught up, and then I'm going back." He really wanted to get through his e-mails and make sure he was ready for the rest of the week, which was bound to be crazy because of all the rescheduled appointments and meetings.

"I'm worried about you. That's all," Jane said.

Ellen joined them. "I canceled the partners' meeting this afternoon, and Carolyn took the Donovan meeting for you. Their appointments were rescheduled. Tomorrow is going to be packed for you, but we tried to keep the other days as normal as possible."

"Thank God," he muttered.

"Also, Gary came by looking for you. I met him in the lobby and explained that you weren't here."

Malcolm looked up and realized that Ellen seemed nervous. "What is it?"

"He seemed different. I was his assistant for three years, and he was never like that." Ellen set down the tablet computer she always carried with her. "He was twitchy and kept looking around like he thought someone was going to jump out at him. Gary was always concerned how everything looked, so his clothes were always immaculate, but he looked schlumpy, and he seems to have lost a lot of weight. He kept wringing his hands and shifting back and forth. When

I told him you weren't here, he demanded to look for you himself. We of course told him that wasn't possible and got him to leave."

"Okay, thank you." The last time he'd seen Gary, he hadn't seemed completely rational to Malcolm either.

"The man I saw isn't the one I used to work for. It's like *Invasion of the Body Snatchers* or something."

Malcolm paused. "I appreciate you letting me know. Please call down to building security and tell them that unless he has a specific invitation, Gary isn't to be allowed up. That should prevent any further incidents." Gary's self-image had always been wrapped up in the firm and his status within it. Malcolm had been rather surprised when he'd resigned, and the more he thought about it, the more he was becoming convinced that it was a bluff Gary hadn't expected to have called. "Thank you both for all your hard work and help. I'll be here for another hour, and then I'm going back to the hospital to sit with Hans."

They both nodded and left his office. Jane looked like she wanted to linger, but Malcolm had too much to do to talk at the moment. He got through his e-mail, forwarding a lot to either Jane or Ellen to follow up on for him. Then he locked his computer and got ready to leave the office.

"Malcolm," Carolyn said as she hurried up to him.

"How did the Donovan meeting go?"

"Wonderfully well. We sold them on the firm, and they have a case that we've already assigned. They were disappointed you weren't there but understood the personal emergency."

"Excellent. Thank you for handling that for me."

"No problem," Carolyn said. Malcolm expected her to move on, but she seemed to have something else she wanted to talk about. "We need to speak about Gary."

Malcolm nodded. "Ellen told me he was here, and she's going to leave an order with building security."

"It isn't that. He's been calling some of our clients, claiming he was treated badly and that he would be better to represent them than we would. He's been blown off by the clients who contacted me, but we need to do something about him. He resigned and wasn't let go, and it was he who treated the rest of us badly."

"What do you suggest?" Malcolm asked.

"We need to get in touch with our clients. I have my people setting up meetings and calls just to reassure them. I suggest the others do the same."

"I agree. I'll have Jane take care of that in the morning. Tell the associates as well. We need to get ahead of this."

"Already done," Carolyn said, and Malcolm thought about what Ellen had said. Maybe Gary really was losing it. This was going to be an annoyance for them, but once word got out, it would ruin Gary. His word would be worth nothing, and no one would take him seriously.

"Excellent." Malcolm turned back to his office and spoke with Jane and Ellen. He figured there was no time like the present. Both were appalled and agreed to set up conference calls to head off any issues. With this crisis under management, he headed out to the hospital.

It was dark outside by the time he pulled into the hospital parking lot. He checked in with the visitors' desk and then went on up. Hans was asleep when he walked into the room. Malcolm sat down as quietly as he could, not wanting to disturb him.

"You're back," Hans said with a slight smile. "The doctor said they got the test results back earlier than expected, and they came back clean. The whole thing was nothing."

"It's better to be sure. If you did have cancer, the earlier they catch it, the better. You'll be healed before you know it, and then you can go back to diving, skiing, and everything you want to do. This will hardly slow you down."

"Did they not catch David's cancer early?"

"He hated doctors, and it wasn't until after he'd been sick for a while that he went. By then there wasn't a whole lot of hope. But he fought as hard as he did everything else." Malcolm took Hans's hand. "Has your ex been back?"

"No." Hans turned to him. "Are you jealous? You sound it."

"He was a real piece of work."

"Yes, he is, and you have nothing to be jealous of." Hans squeezed slightly. "They brought me dinner, and it was bland and terrible."

"Tomorrow after work I'll cook you a nice dinner. I promise. Call me and let me know when they're going to discharge you, and I'll come pick you up."

"Erik and Chris stopped by a little while ago, and Erik said he'd pick me up tomorrow. I figured that way you wouldn't have to leave work, especially after you spent all day today here with me."

"Then I'll come to your house after work, make you dinner, and help look after you."

"I'm not going to be an invalid."

"Probably not, but you're going to hurt like hell for a few days, and moving will be difficult." Malcolm leaned closer and lowered his voice. "Just smile and say thank you. And if you're good, I'll even stay and take care of you well into the night."

Hans groaned deeply. "That's so not fair. It hurts when I laugh… or try to move like that."

"Then get some rest, because you know you're going to need it." Malcolm was aching to get a look at Hans, from head to toe, to make sure he was truly okay. This whole scare had pulled the rug out from under him, and he wanted to get it back where it belonged. They both did. And they needed some quiet time alone. Malcolm knew Hans wasn't going to be up for anything strenuous, but that didn't mean he didn't need to be taken care of.

"Damn," Hans whimpered as Malcolm lightly stroked his arm, trying to soothe and relax him rather than excite him at this point. There would be plenty of time for that once he got him home. "Did you mean what you said earlier, or was I all loopy and imagining the whole thing?"

"What exactly might it have been that you imagined?" Malcolm asked teasingly.

"I think when I was coming out of anesthesia, once you had scared Troy away, you said something, and I want to know if it was real."

"Uh-huh. Do you remember what you said?" Malcolm leaned a little closer, lightly nuzzling Hans's neck.

"Yeah, I do. But I may have been saying it because of an anesthetic delusion."

"It was real," Malcolm told him. "It was very real, and I know you said it to me. I wasn't delusional." He brought Hans's hand to his lips, lightly kissing the back of his fingers. "I can't believe you actually feel that way sometimes, and I keep wondering what I could have done to make a hot guy like you fall in love with me. But I learned not to question the good things in life, otherwise they tend to evaporate."

"I do, so you need to get used to it. Age really doesn't matter."

"You do know that I won't be able to keep up with you. You'll be out tearing up the slopes or diving the deepest wreck, and I'll still be on the bunny hill or in the kiddie diving pool."

"You don't have to go everywhere with me. It would be nice if you try some things, like diving. But if we go someplace warm and I'm diving, you can do what you like, and I'll look forward to seeing you when I get back. I know you and David did a lot together, but we can have our separate interests. Not all of us are daredevils of that sort." Hans smiled a little, and then his eyes began to close. "I'm sorry I'm so tired."

"It's all right. Go to sleep." Malcolm sat back, and Hans dozed. He knew that surgery took a lot out of a person, and the anesthetic's effects could linger. Malcolm stayed for a few hours, talking softly when Hans was awake. He left when it seemed that Hans was completely wearing out.

At home, he pulled into his usual spot and got out of the car. It was snowing, and everything looked clean with a fresh coating of white. He went up his walk, remembering that he was going to need to shovel in the morning.

"What the heck?" he said out loud as he noticed fresh footprints in the snow up near the house. They went around toward the back door, and it seemed someone had been trying to look inside. Malcolm followed the footprints around through the gate, which had been opened against the snow, and around to the back door. Nothing seemed disturbed, and the back storm door didn't seem to have been opened.

He unlocked the door and went inside, listening for anything out of the ordinary. He heard nothing other than the hum of the refrigerator and the soft whoosh as the furnace kicked in. Malcolm closed the door and took off his shoes, continuing to listen. He pulled out his phone and slowly went through the house. It didn't seem like anyone had been inside, and he made sure all the doors were locked before going upstairs. Once he was sure that the house was secure and that no one was inside, he got cleaned up and went to bed, but he didn't sleep much. Between his concern for Hans and the footprints outside, he woke at the smallest sound.

Chapter 9

"HOW WAS your day?" Hans asked when Malcolm stepped into his house the following evening after work. He sat on the sofa with a blanket over his legs.

"I never had a spare second. Gary has been making trouble, so I've been contacting clients in between nearly back-to-back meetings all day." Malcolm had a pile of work to get done, and it wasn't going to do itself, but he could barely keep his eyes open. Before stopping at Hans's, he'd gone by his house to check on it. Nothing had seemed amiss, and there were no additional footprints outside. He figured maybe someone had had the wrong house or something. "How are you feeling? I see you're sitting up."

"I'm tired of lying down and doing nothing. I know I have to rest, but it's driving me crazy."

Malcolm took off his coat and hung it up, then approached Hans and gingerly kissed him. "I brought some things for dinner. It's not what I originally intended to make. I wasn't expecting to be this late." Though he should have known—after being off for a day, things had really piled up.

"It's all right. I haven't been really hungry up until now."

Malcolm helped Hans lie down and then went into the kitchen to start the pasta. He wanted something that wouldn't be too heavy. It wasn't too long before he had the pasta cooking and the meat for the sauce browning. He made some garlic bread as well, and almost by accident, everything was ready at the same time. He checked the living room and found Hans asleep on the sofa. He'd been about to ask if Hans wanted to come into the kitchen, but he brought the food in to him and set it on the table.

Hans's incredible eyes fluttered open, and he slowly sat back up. Malcolm brought him some water to drink and then joined him, sitting next to him.

Malcolm couldn't believe how happy he was. Now that he'd finally figured out how to just let go and stop worrying about every little thing, he was truly happy. "I was thinking that in a few months, we could go on vacation if you like. I'm already sick of winter, and maybe somewhere warm with water would be a lot of fun."

"You could learn to dive if you like," Hans said. "If we choose a resort, some of them offer diving lessons. You won't believe how amazing it is under the water."

Malcolm leaned closer. "I'll try just about anything as long as I'm with you." He was a little nervous about being underwater like that, but he was also excited about learning something new.

"Let's plan something for early May, if that works for you. My manuscript has to be in by then, so a trip would be a reward for getting that done. Lord knows you deserve a vacation. Will that give you enough time to prepare?"

"Yeah."

"Awesome. Then when I get a chance I'll come up with some possibilities and we can pick one you like. I'm thinking maybe a week on a small resort on Bonaire. They have some of the world's best diving. But we can look at other places too." Hans took a few bites of his dinner and then talked about reefs and corals, turtles, and everything else they might see.

In the end he ate about half of his food before he began to tire. Malcolm finished his own dinner and took care of the dishes. By the time he was done, Hans was asleep again. He sat with him, reading some papers from work, and then helped Hans into bed. He was about to leave, but Hans took his hand, and Malcolm took off his shoes and climbed into bed next to him, carefully holding Hans through the night.

"How is it going contacting our clients?" Malcolm asked the following morning at a brief partners' meeting.

"Mine were pleased about the communication," Howard said, "and even the clients I took over from Gary want to stay with the firm. They feel they'll get better representation with us than with Gary." He seemed inordinately pleased.

"I found the same thing," Lyndon added. "No one wants to go with Gary. I had one client tell me that the only reason they worked with Gary was because they knew he'd have the support of the rest of the firm."

"I also think we need to change the name of the firm," Howard suggested. "We need to remove Hanlan from the letterhead. I know we kept it because of Gary's father, but I think it needs to go after this."

Malcolm nodded. "Okay. Let's table the name change until next week and make sure we follow up with our associates and finish this out. I want to put this to bed and get on with business. We have the potential for a lot more business coming our way, and we have a new associate starting next week with some experience in literary and entertainment contracts, so we can start promoting that growing portion of our business as well. Are there any other issues or concerns?" Malcolm asked and received head shakes in return. "Just a note that our newest partner will be buying in next month, so we'll have a new face at this table very soon." He stood and left the conference room to get back to work.

Malcolm had intended to take his lunch in his office but decided to go get something instead. He needed a few minutes out of the office, so he went down to the sandwich shop in the lobby.

"What are you doing to me?" Gary called angrily as he strode across the lobby toward Malcolm. "My clients have been leaving me right and left, and I have nothing!"

As he approached, Malcolm took a step back. Gary was disheveled, he hadn't shaved, and Malcolm saw what Ellen had told him about the day before. His eyes were a little wild, and he was speaking way too loudly.

"You went after our clients with a lie. You could have left well enough alone, but you didn't. You always thought you were the heart of the firm, but you aren't. And it turns out even your own clients aren't happy with you. So there's nothing I can do. We'll protect our clients, and that includes from you. So I think it's best you leave before I call security. You aren't allowed in this building any longer."

"I'm looking at space here."

"Not when I explain to the landlords that it's either us or you," Malcolm answered calmly. "So I suggest you leave." He glanced at the guards, who were taking an interest in their conversation, and stepped back. The guards came over. "Please escort Mr. Hanlan from the building." He watched while they removed Gary.

Malcolm decided he wasn't particularly hungry and went back into the office elevators without bothering to get a sandwich. Instead he went right up to his office and closed the door. He wasn't in the mood to be disturbed until his next appointment.

"BEING SENIOR partner is turning into a major pain in the ass, and everyone looks to me to solve their problems for them. If they'd think, they could do it for themselves, but it's like half the people have turned their brains off," Malcolm groused as he sat down at Hans's table. He'd brought Chinese because once again he'd been running late, and he didn't want Hans cooking. He needed to rest. Of course, Hans was going even more stir-crazy and had been trying to work on his manuscript, which had only left him looking more tired and drawn.

"I'm fine, Malcolm. You don't need to look at me as though I'm about to keel over at any second."

"I'm just worried." Malcolm stabbed a bite of his sweet and sour and popped it into his mouth. "After dinner I'll go home."

"Don't," Hans said. "I want you to stay."

"I need some clothes to wear in the morning."

"Then we can ride over. I need to get out for a little, and you can bring some things back." Hans took a bite of his Mongolian beef and smiled. "Maybe we could get frozen custard for dessert while we're out. I saw online that Kopp's has strawberry today, and I love that."

"Okay." Malcolm knew when he was beaten, not that he really minded. Frozen custard wasn't good for his waistline, but as a treat it was wonderful. "Let's finish eating and we'll go, but you have to promise to take it easy, and we'll drive through to get the custard."

Hans growled but didn't argue, and once they were done and Malcolm had taken care of all the trash and dishes, they got ready to go outside. Malcolm started the car to get it warm, and then Hans joined him and they rode the few miles to Malcolm's house.

Everything looked the same. There didn't seem to be any new tracks in the snow around the house, but it was hard to be sure since there hadn't been fresh snow. They walked to the front door together, and Malcolm unlocked it, letting them both inside. "Go on and sit in the living room. I'll get some clothes and change out of these. Then we can get you that custard." He took off his overcoat, draped it over the nearest chair, and went upstairs.

It didn't take him long to pack a small bag and get a fresh suit for the morning. He'd used the change of clothes he kept at the office, so he grabbed an extra suit, adding it to the bag before coming downstairs.

He reached the bottom of the stairs, peering into the living room. The handle of the bag in his right hand slipped from his grip, and the bag hit the floor. It took him all of three seconds to realize that Gary was standing in his living room, and that he had a gun and was pointing it at Hans.

"There you are," Gary said, turning around slowly, his eyes red and wild beyond belief. "I was keeping your boyfriend company until you got back." He took a step back, probably to where he could still see Hans, but the gun was now pointed at Malcolm.

Malcolm knew exactly where it was pointed. He could feel the heat rising from that very spot in the center of his chest. "Why are you doing this?"

"You took away everything," Gary said. "I was senior partner, and now you are. I bet you orchestrated that whole thing."

"I supported you, remember?" Malcolm said, his leg shaking until he got it under control. "You don't want to do this. Hurting me won't change anything, and it's going to make things worse for you. Just put the gun down and go. No one is going to follow you, and we can forget this ever happened."

"I can't. There's nothing left. My ex-wife found out about my job, and she's trying to keep me from seeing my kids since I can't pay the support any longer. I'm fucking broke, no job, and I'm the laughingstock of the legal community because of your little campaign to discredit me. No one will hire me, and I can't even start my own practice because I have no clients."

"We can help you," Malcolm said, trying to think of something to say to calm him down.

"No, you can't. Everything is ruined. I'm done, and I'm going to take you down with me."

The gun shook a little, and then Gary took a step forward. Malcolm thought he saw Hans move in his peripheral vision, but he kept his gaze square on Gary.

"Just put the gun down. Nothing is so bad that you can't figure out a solution." Malcolm knew he had to keep Gary talking.

"No one can figure this out. I was supposed to be senior partner just like my father. Fuck, that was all my dad ever pushed me toward. Law school, then into the practice. After he retired, he pushed me to work harder so I could be senior. That was the last thing the fucker said to me. Well, I'll let you in on a little secret. I never wanted to go to law school. I wanted to be a painter or do something with my hands. The law is so fucking boring I can't stand it, but my dad refused to pay for anything else, so here I fucking am. I hate my father, and I wish I'd told him to go fuck himself years ago."

Malcolm listened. "I'm sorry about that. Your father could be demanding."

He wanted to sound sympathetic and keep Gary's attention on him and away from Hans. That was all he could think of. Malcolm took a step backward and then another, moving farther from Gary and hoping Gary would mimic him. He did, putting a little more space between him and Hans.

"But this isn't the answer. Your father is dead, and you can be your own man. There are a lot of things you can do if you don't want to practice law. Go into business or work for a corporation. They always need good people. You have experience and a track record."

For a few seconds Gary's hand wavered, and Malcolm thought he'd gotten through to him, but then Gary's expression hardened and he thrust the gun forward.

"I know what you're doing, and it isn't going to work. I have nothing to live for, and I'm going to take you with me." Gary tensed.

Malcolm thought quickly. "What about your children? How are they going to feel when you're gone? You're their daddy, and that's more important than any job. They need you and will need you for a long time. You don't want them to grow up without a father, do you?"

"They deserve a better father than me," Gary said, clearly flustered.

"They only get one father, and they need you more than you realize." Malcolm hoped like hell that he was onto something. He was out of ideas and strongly felt that Gary was going to shoot at any moment. He also knew that if Gary shot him, he'd do the same to Hans and then most likely take his own life. "Your children deserve to have a dad."

Gary inhaled deeply, clearly weighing his words. Malcolm took a step closer. "Just give me the gun and then go home and call your children." He hoped Gary was seeing some sort of reason.

"I can't," he said, near tears.

Malcolm knew he was nearing the moment of final decision. "Yes, you can. Just give me the gun, and then you can go." Malcolm did his best to keep calm even though he was seconds from wetting himself.

"No, I can't," Gary said, his gaze becoming focused. "It's time to end this. I'm worth more dead than alive, and my kids will be taken care of."

He raised the gun, and Malcolm closed his eyes. A bang rang through the house, followed by a thud. Malcolm checked himself over, expecting pain, but there was none. Maybe he was already dead. Slowly he opened his eyes and saw Hans standing over Gary.

"I hope that paperweight wasn't important," Hans said as shards of glass sparkled on the floor. "I threw it and hit him on the back of the head." Hans pulled his phone out of his pocket and called 911, then explained what happened and told them to come right away.

Malcolm watched Gary, but he didn't seem to be moving. He did groan a few times, so Malcolm knew he was alive, but that was all. The gun had slid into the kitchen, and Malcolm kicked the door closed. "Are you okay?" he asked Hans, not wanting to move too much so he wouldn't disturb anything or grind glass into his floors.

"Yes. Are you?" Hans asked.

"Yes. Just stay where you are. There's glass everywhere, and if Gary tries to get up, I'll take care of him." He bent down as Gary began to shift his arms to get them under him. "Move and I'll use your head for a soccer ball," he growled at Gary, who stilled.

Sirens blared, and the front door opened, police streaming in, guns in hand. They stopped when they saw Gary on the floor.

Malcolm pointed toward the door. "His gun is in there. There's glass everywhere, so be careful, and I'd really appreciate it if you'd take this sad pile of trash out of my house." He had had more of Gary in the last few days than he wanted for the rest of his life.

"Who called us?" the officer in charge asked with a steady gaze that brooked no bullshit.

"I did," Hans said. "He broke in and held me at gunpoint until Malcolm came downstairs. Then he threatened both of us. Malcolm was able to occupy his attention, and when Gary was about to shoot, I knocked him out with a glass paperweight. That's where the glass came from."

"No one has touched the gun except him. Fingerprint analysis will confirm that. His name is Gary Hanlan. He was a partner in my law firm until he resigned." Malcolm tossed Hans his phone. "Call Lyndon—he's in there—and ask him to come right over."

"Who is Lyndon?" the officer asked.

"My attorney," Malcolm answered. He had no intention of letting anyone put either him or Hans through any bullshit.

"And you are?"

"Malcolm Webber, senior partner at Warren, Hanlan, and Webber."

That had the desired effect.

"We have touched nothing, and I'll allow you to gather whatever evidence you need."

"Well, thank you." He didn't sound remotely amused. "If you want, you can join him in the living room."

He motioned one of the other officers into the kitchen, presumably to get the gun, and Malcolm joined Hans, sitting on the arm of the chair and taking Hans's hand. The officers handcuffed Gary and picked him up off the floor, removing him from the house.

"All I could think of was keeping him away from you," Malcolm told Hans.

"And I was trying to figure out how to call the police without him knowing. Then, when he was about to shoot, I grabbed the only thing I could think of to throw at him. I got lucky and hit him on the back of the head, and he went down like a ton of bricks."

"Where did you learn to throw like that?"

"When I was in Africa. I wanted to have one of the heroes in one of my early books subdue the killer with an old-fashioned sling. The idea was to do sort of a historical adventure. Part of my research was in basic weapons, and I learned how to throw with accuracy. I haven't done it in a while, but I guess I remembered when it counted." Hans held him closer. "How did you know to talk to him like that?"

"I had to try to calm him and see if he'd surrender on his own."

The officer turned back to them. "Gentlemen, I'm Detective Rodriguez, and I'd like to ask you both a few questions."

"Our attorney is on the way," Malcolm said.

"We just need to know what happened," he persisted.

"Gary broke into my house and held us at gunpoint. I tried to talk him down, and Hans made one hell of a shot with a glass paperweight and took him out."

"Did he say why he was here?"

"He was senior partner but was removed a few weeks ago. He also resigned from the firm, and things have been going very badly for him since. He was acting erratically at the office, and I think he intended to shoot us and then take his own life. He blamed me for his troubles."

"But you were the one who got him elected senior partner in the first place," Hans said.

"True, but I'm also the one who replaced him, and when Gary went after our clients, we shut him out. He had nothing left and couldn't take it." That was all Malcolm intended to say until Lyndon arrived.

"You threw the paperweight?" Detective Rodriguez asked, turning to Hans.

"Yes. In Malcolm's defense, and I'd do it again. He had Malcolm at gunpoint."

"You are?"

"Hans Erickson, Malcolm's boyfriend," Hans said. "I'm a writer."

Detective Rodriguez blinked a few times. "Not *the* Hans Erickson?"

Hans nodded.

"I love your work. I've read *Diving the Storm* twice, and I gave a copy to my son. It's awesome."

"Thank you," Hans said quietly. "I never expected my research to come in handy in such a practical way."

"We've arrested Mr. Hanlan and will charge him. I'll need to take some information and have you both make statements. It's pretty clear what happened, and your stories are supported by the evidence."

"Is Gary talking?" Malcolm asked.

"All we're getting out of him right now is gibberish. Maybe the conk on the head scrambled his brains. He's being transported to the hospital. An ambulance is on its way."

"You might have someone see if they can match his shoes with tracks in the snow around the house. I noticed them the other day, and in hindsight he may have been watching the house, looking for me."

He made notes. "We'll do what we can," he agreed as Lyndon came inside.

"What happened?"

"Gary's cheese fell off his cracker, and he tried to kill Malcolm," Hans answered. "He held us at gunpoint, and I took him out with a paperweight."

"We've cooperated with the police, and they've been good," Malcolm said. He'd contacted Lyndon as a precaution in case the police got everything messed up.

"We'll need both of you to make a statement, and we're going to get Mr. Hanlan some medical attention. He'll be in custody the entire time," Detective Rodriguez said as flashes went off in the hallway.

The police took photographs in the house, and everyone stayed clear and let them do their jobs. Finally the police finished and got ready to leave.

"We got a few good prints in the snow, and they match Mr. Hanlan's boots."

Malcolm nodded, relieved that he had an answer as to who had been outside the house.

"We'll arrange to come down tomorrow to sign statements and press charges," Lyndon told the detective and walked out with him.

"That was enough excitement to last a lifetime," Malcolm told Hans once it was just the two of them.

"Yeah. That's a new one. And you were so calm—it was impressive."

"I was shaking like a leaf."

"But it didn't show. All those years in court and in front of clients really paid off. You looked calm and collected. Gary didn't have a chance," Hans said.

"He was going to shoot. And who knows what might have happened if it hadn't been for you?" He leaned closer to Hans, holding him and sitting still. This whole thing was overwhelming, and everything that had happened slammed into him all at once. Now that it was over, fear welled up inside. Malcolm shivered and shook for a few minutes. "Gary was going to kill me. I could see it in his eyes. He intended to shoot any second."

"I know. I saw him get ready and had to act." Hans shook as well, and they held each other.

"The last thing I ever expected was to be held at gunpoint." He was a tax attorney, for God's sake. Granted, he dealt with people who tried to cheat on their taxes all the time, but it wasn't like he defended hardened criminals.

"It's going to be fine. Gary is in custody, and he isn't going anywhere."

"His lawyer will try to get him out on bail," Malcolm said. "That's what he does."

"Maybe. But I'd think that would be hard. He's been showing signs of mental instability. Make sure you make that clear when you give your statement so that the police can request that he be held as a danger to himself as well as others."

"I'll have to talk to Ellen. She noticed it as well." Malcolm's mind was already working toward how he could build a case. "Maybe there are others who can help." He had no intention of allowing Gary to go free if he could help it. There was little doubt in his mind that Gary would come after him and Hans again if he were allowed to go free once more. He'd been so fixated on him and the perceived slights Malcolm had caused.

"Don't worry about that now. He's not in any shape to go anywhere at the moment, and he isn't going to be for a while. He was hit pretty hard. I hope I didn't hurt him too badly. I mean, he is a real prick and I hope he ends up in jail for a damn long time, but I don't want to be the one who scrambled his brains."

"You sure have a colorful way with words at a time like this."

"I'm a writer, and I get a little giddy when my life has been threatened. Sue me." Hans flashed a nervous smile.

"Never say that to a lawyer." Malcolm was pleased that he could tell a small joke of his own, and it made some of the tension that had settled on his shoulders fall away.

The front door opened and closed, and Lyndon came back into the room. "I think this is going to be a pretty open-and-shut case. The police are convinced that your stories are true and that Gary was the aggressor. I don't expect any repercussions from you throwing the paperweight to subdue him. After all, you were in Malcolm's home with his permission and Gary was not. I'm going to go back home. Give me a call if you need anything, and I'll work everything out tomorrow so you can give your statements. Other than that, I suggest the two of you try to relax and get some rest."

"We will, thanks," Malcolm said, getting up and walking Lyndon to the door. "I appreciate everything."

"No problem," Lyndon said with a sly grin. "Hans seems like a nice guy, and he sure has one hell of an arm."

"He's an incredible man who surprises me all the time."

"That's good." Lyndon leaned back, presumably so he could see Hans once again. "You two have a good night."

"We'll try," Malcolm said and opened the door, thanking Lyndon one more time. He watched until Lyndon got to his car before closing the door.

"Do you want to go or stay here?" Hans asked.

Malcolm had completely forgotten about their plans to stay at Hans's. "Let me get the bags and clean up this mess a little before we get out of here." He got a broom and swept up the glass, then threw it in the trash. Then he grabbed his bags, placing them near the door before helping Hans get to his feet.

They left the house, and Malcolm locked the door. They rode to Hans's house in near silence. Malcolm couldn't help ruminating over what could have happened.

"I fully expected him to shoot," he said quietly just before turning into the driveway. "You should have gotten away if you could have." Malcolm pulled the car to a stop.

"Did you think I was going to let that bastard take you and not do something about it?" Hans snapped. "Are you daft? Because that wasn't going to happen." Hans took his hand as soon as Malcolm turned off the engine. "What the hell is wrong, Malcolm? You look like I just told you that the moon is made of cheese."

"I do believe you. I don't understand why."

Hans pulled his hand away and got out of the car, then closed his door with more force than necessary. Malcolm watched him walk across the headlight beams and then go into the house. He wondered if he should go home. He was tired beyond belief, and this whole thing with Gary had left him feeling older than he had in a very long time. He cared about Hans, and yes, he loved him, but he hadn't been able to protect him.

A tap on the window brought his attention to Hans.

"Are you coming inside?" Hans asked when Malcolm lowered the glass.

Malcolm opened the door and got out, then lifted his bags from the backseat. "Maybe I should go home and let you get some rest."

Hans stepped closer. "Maybe you should stop thinking about whatever is rolling around in that brilliant mind of yours and come inside." Hans stepped back, pulling Malcolm along with his intense gaze.

Malcolm closed the car doors and followed Hans back into the house.

"You really need to let go of this age thing. It's not an issue to anyone except you." Hans closed the door. "Unless of course I'm not mature enough for you and you really need someone your own age."

Malcolm set the bags on the sofa. "I couldn't protect you from Gary."

"First, neither of us knew we needed protecting from the little nutball. And second, this is a relationship. We're not cavemen, and

I'm not the little woman who needs to be taken care of. In case you haven't realized it, we worked together. You held Gary's attention so he wasn't watching me the whole time, and I was able to take him out. I'd say that was pretty special."

Malcolm couldn't argue with that. "But I have to ask you something. I'm a decade older than you. That means that there's every chance I'll get sick eventually, and you'll need to take care of me. I did that for David because I loved him, but it was the hardest thing I ever had to do. And I don't want you to have to do that for me. It ripped my heart out every day to see him slipping further and further away from me by inches. I don't want to have to go through that again, and I don't want someone I love to have to do that for me."

"You know that doesn't matter."

"But it does. I watched David die slowly, and it nearly killed me."

"Malcolm," Hans said gently. "We don't get to choose what happens to us, including whether we get cancer or some other disease. That's all part of life. You know that. But if you stop living, then you're giving up on everything and everyone, and I doubt that's what you want."

"I don't. I've been happy. You make me happy, and I love you for bringing joy back to my life. But what if it ends?"

"And what if it doesn't?" Hans countered. "What if we get another twenty or thirty years together, and then we both die in our sleep because of some rare disease that only two people who love each other can get that makes them die at the same time?" Hans was being silly, but he was trying to make a point, so Malcolm kept his mouth shut. "Does it really matter?"

Malcolm had to admit that it really didn't, because the thought of going home and leaving Hans behind made his heart ache and ice water race through his veins. "I don't want it to."

"Then it doesn't. It's as simple as that. Because I love you too, and I think you're sexy, fun, and amazing to talk with, and I want to spend years getting to know you. I think it will take that long."

Malcolm carefully hugged Hans to him. "I want that too." He was finding it hard to believe that this was actually happening to him.

"Well, let's get your things put in my room, and then we can go to bed."

"Are you aching?" Malcolm asked, concerned that they'd done too much and had aggravated Hans's wound.

"I am," Hans said, lifting his gaze until it met Malcolm's, and the heat he saw took Malcolm's breath away. "I'm wanting and aching so badly I don't know how I can go another minute without you, and I'm going to feel the same way in a decade."

Any feeble argument Malcolm might have put forward was swept aside when Hans kissed him, pressing their bodies together. The wind outside whipped around the house, rattling the windows, but they were warm together in a cocoon that surrounded only the two of them. The kiss grew more heated, and Malcolm carefully guided Hans down the hallway toward the bedroom.

Undressing wasn't elegant or some gorgeous expression of love. It was two people, one moving very carefully, removing their clothes and getting under the covers. Malcolm made sure Hans was settled and comfortable before bringing his lips in contact with his amazing chest. He sucked at a flat pink nipple, loving the way Hans squirmed under him. "I want you more than I can say. I came close to losing you today," Malcolm whispered next to Hans's lips.

"You know the feeling's mutual. I watched you with him and wanted to rip Gary limb from limb. All I could think about was what I'd do if he took you away from me." Hans closed the distance between their lips, and the thinking portion of the evening was over.

Malcolm kept his weight off Hans while working his lips down his luscious body, careful of the bandage at his side. He drove Hans to a whining, quivering mass. He loved that he could do that. Hans was a big man, strong, with rippling muscles. Looking at him was enough to steal the air from the room for Malcolm. "I want to make love to you, but I'm scared of hurting you." Malcolm swirled his tongue on Hans's navel.

"You'd never hurt me, and I've been waiting for that for a while." Hans carefully rolled onto his side, and Malcolm pressed to his back, holding him gently.

"Are you sure?" Malcolm asked and leaned forward, licking and sucking Hans's neck softly. "Your scent drives me crazy." He pressed his hips to Hans's butt, sliding his cock along his crack as he slid his hands down Hans's side and across to his cock, gripping and stroking him as he shuddered against him. This was so intimate and heart touching. They didn't have to do anything more than this to make his heart soar. Hans here with him, whole, disease-free, and this was all he could ever want.

"Yes. I'm always sure with you." Hans groaned as Malcolm gripped him tight, stroking the way he'd learned Hans liked, with just the right amount of pressure.

Malcolm thrust his hips, sliding his cock between Hans's buttcheeks. Hans pressed back, adding to the sensation and intensity. Holding Hans in his hand, all silky heat, was always incredible. "You feel so good everywhere." Malcolm sucked at Hans's ear. His intention was to drive Hans crazy, but the effect was to do the same to himself, especially with the way Hans filled his ears with a symphony of steady moans that grew in intensity and volume, telling Malcolm that he was getting closer and closer to pushing Hans over the edge and threatening to carry himself along for the ride.

"Damn it," Hans groaned, pushing back against him, then thrusting his hips forward. "I want… need…."

"I know what you want, and you can take it all. Whatever you need is yours." He stroked faster, tighter, and Hans groaned louder, throbbing and pulsing in his hand.

"On the edge… please… just…."

"I know." Malcolm was quickly getting beyond words as well. His own excitement grew and grew. He was going to tumble off the edge, and he needed Hans to go first. Malcolm held his own pleasure at bay, adding speed and friction until Hans inhaled deeply, moaned loudly, and stilled.

Hans came in a rush, yelling at the top of his lungs, pushing Malcolm back and to the very precipice of passion before he too rolled down the other side in an uncontrolled freight train of heat. Malcolm stilled and held Hans as he floated. He hoped like hell he hadn't hurt him.

After a few minutes, Hans slowly rolled over and pulled Malcolm toward him until their faces were inches apart. "God, I love you. I don't know if I said it before so plainly, but I do. You make me happy."

Malcolm blinked a few times. "I love you too." He had never in a million years expected to be able to say those words to another human being again. "You make me feel alive—no, because of you, I'm awake again, really awake, and I can't thank you enough."

"How about when I feel better, you thank me properly and energetically?" Hans stroked Malcolm's cheek lightly.

Malcolm shifted, letting Hans roll onto his back. "How about I thank you many times for the rest of our lives?"

"I can live with that." Hans pulled him down into a kiss.

Epilogue

A year later

IT WAS the coldest day of the entire damned year. The wind howled as the sun blazed in its glory before going down. Clear skies always meant blistering cold, and tonight was going to be no exception. "This is it," Hans said as he joined Malcolm outside the house he and David had shared, carrying the very last box. "We can put this in the spare room for now."

"Yes, though it's getting full." Malcolm locked the door and turned to look up at the front of the house. Tomorrow he'd give the key to the real estate agent, and that would be the end of it. A young couple with a newborn was due to move in tomorrow, and the house would be filled with life and love once again. That made leaving so much easier.

"It won't be for too long," Hans said as he headed toward the car, placed the box in the trunk, and closed the lid. "I wish the deal on the new house could have closed a little earlier so we could have brought your things right over there."

"It's the way of things. Thankfully your house will close a few weeks after we get the new one, so we can move our things after doing some of the projects we want to get done.

"After we get moved in, I was thinking that we could take a much deserved vacation. Say in late April. You'll be done with the book you're working on, we'll be settled in, and we could fly down to Bonaire for some dive time."

Hans came around the car and moved right into his arms. "That's perfect. I know an amazing small resort, and I'll book diving classes for you." Hans kissed him. "You won't believe the wonders in store."

Malcolm slipped his arms under Hans's coat, cupping his tight butt. "Speaking of wonders...." He kissed Hans hard, and his body reacted with gusto.

Over the last year they had grown closer and closer, spending time at both houses. It quickly got to be too much, and in the end they decided to sell both of them and buy a home they could enjoy together. One that would be theirs together. The decision had been a hard one for Malcolm, and he'd gone back and forth with it for a few days. In the end, he decided selling the house was more about starting a new life with Hans than it was about saying good-bye to David.

They parted, and Malcolm turned to look at the house once more.

"You know David will always be with you, regardless of where you live."

"I know." The ache that usually settled in his gut when he thought about David didn't this time. Instead he felt warm in a way the cold wind couldn't touch. David was with him, and he liked to think that David would be pleased he'd found happiness again. "It feels like I'm saying a last good-bye to him."

"Maybe you are," Hans said. "You're certainly different from the man I first met. You're confident and settled in the life we're building."

"I know, and it's going to be good." Malcolm didn't worry over things the way he had. "And I'm looking forward to trying new things again."

"Is that the reason for the trip?" Hans asked, his hands wandering under Malcolm's coat.

"Yes and no. I'm fifty-three years old, and I remember a few weeks ago waking up in bed after you completely wore me out, and I asked myself what I was waiting for. If I don't do the things I want and take a chance now, I may never be able to. I work hard, and I plan for the future. David and I both did that, and what did it get us? David still got cancer and died, and we didn't get to do all the things we'd talked about. That isn't going to happen again. So I'm going to learn to scuba dive, and maybe you and I will go on a camera safari. I want to climb a mountain in the Alps and look down on the world."

"You are not climbing Everest, though. Even I have my limits."

"Probably not. But I understand that there are some archeological digs that we can go be part of. I bet that would make some great fodder for your stories. Fossil hunt in the Dakotas, explore parts of Alaska."

"You have quite a list," Hans said. "I like it."

"Me too." Now that he thought about it, there were so many possibilities that were open to him.

"What about work while you're off doing all these things?" Hans asked.

"I'm making a good salary as senior partner, and the business is growing. We've decided to offer William Fisher a partnership. You've met him a few times."

"Young, focused, and intense."

"That's him. He's earned it, and I'm going to turn over some of my less demanding clients to him. He'll do a very good job, and I'll still be there to consult."

"What about Ellen?" Hans asked as he moved away, and Malcolm pulled his coat closed, walking around the car to get in.

"She's going to be his assistant, and Jane will remain mine." Everything was working out as far as Malcolm could see. "So I can take vacations and not work myself into an early grave."

"I like the sound of that." Hans pulled open the passenger door and got into the car. Malcolm heard the door close, but he stood in his open door for a few seconds, taking one last look at the house.

"I know," Malcolm said out loud, his voice carried on the wind. It was indeed time. "I got lucky twice." He blinked a couple of times and then got into the car. He pulled the door closed, leaned across the seat to Hans, and shared a kiss that heated quickly. He reluctantly broke the kiss, started the engine, and pulled away from the curb, squeezing Hans's hand with excitement.

ANDREW GREY grew up in western Michigan with a father who loved to tell stories and a mother who loved to read them. Since then he has lived all over the country and traveled throughout the world. He has a master's degree from the University of Wisconsin-Milwaukee and now works full-time on his writing. Andrew's hobbies include collecting antiques, gardening, and leaving his dirty dishes anywhere but in the sink (particularly when writing). He considers himself blessed with an accepting family, fantastic friends, and the world's most supportive and loving husband. Andrew currently lives in beautiful historic Carlisle, Pennsylvania.

E-mail: andrewgrey@comcast.net
Website: www.andrewgreybooks.com

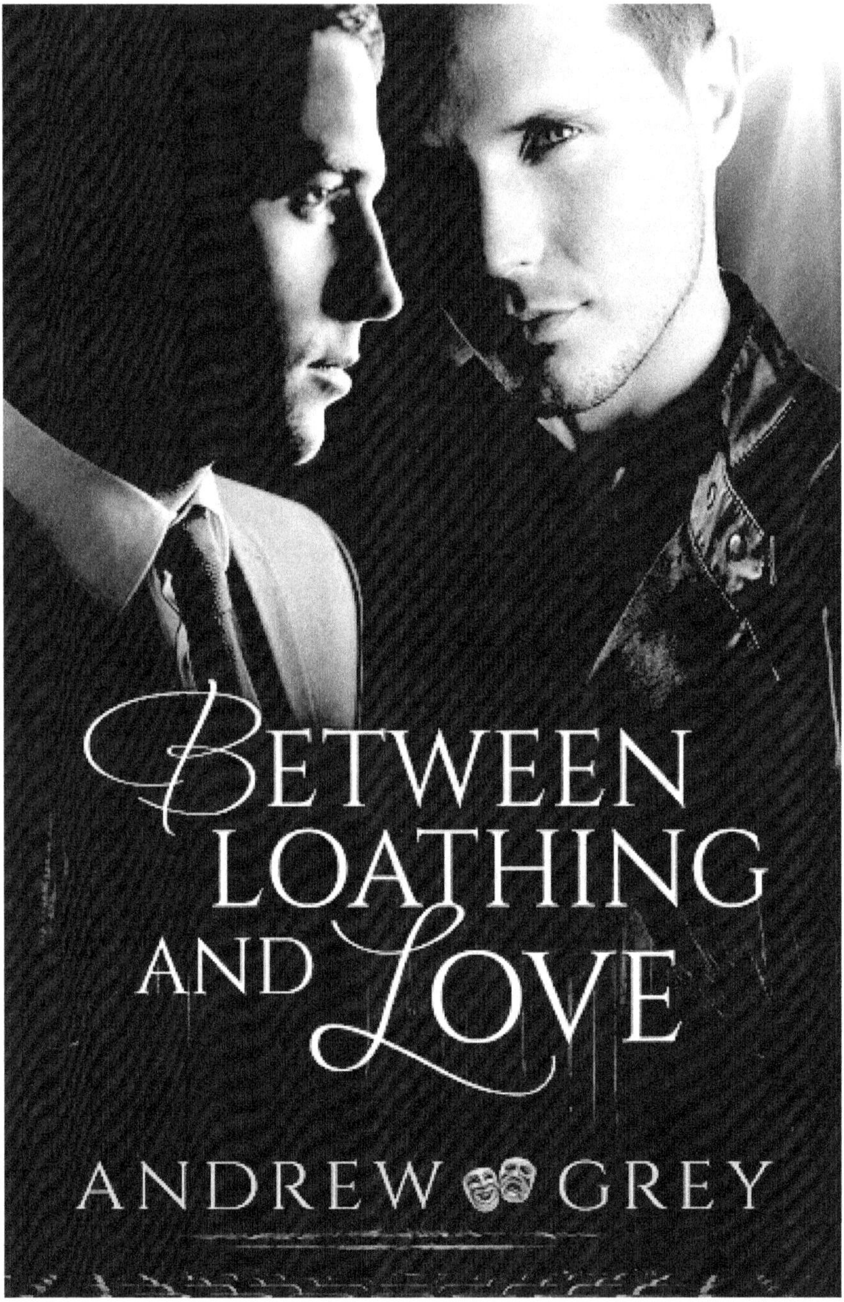
BETWEEN
LOATHING
AND LOVE
ANDREW GREY

Theatrical agent Payton Gowan meets with former classmate—and prospective client—Beckett Huntington with every intention of brushing him off. Beckett not only made high school a living hell for Payton, but he was also responsible for dashing Payton's dreams of becoming a Broadway star.

Aspiring actor Beckett Huntington arrives in New York City on a wing and a prayer, struggling to land his first gig. He knows scoring Payton Gowan as an agent would be a great way to get his foot in the door, but with their history, getting the chance is going to be a tough sell.

Against Payton's better judgment, he agrees to give Beckett a chance, only to discover—to his amazement—that Beckett actually does have talent.

Payton signs Beckett but can't trust him—until Payton's best friend, Val, is attacked. When Beckett is there for him, Payton begins to see another side to his former bully. Amidst attempts by a jealous agent to sabotage Beckett's career and tear apart their blossoming love, Payton and Beckett must learn to let go of the past if they have any chance at playing out a future together.

www.dreamspinnerpress.com

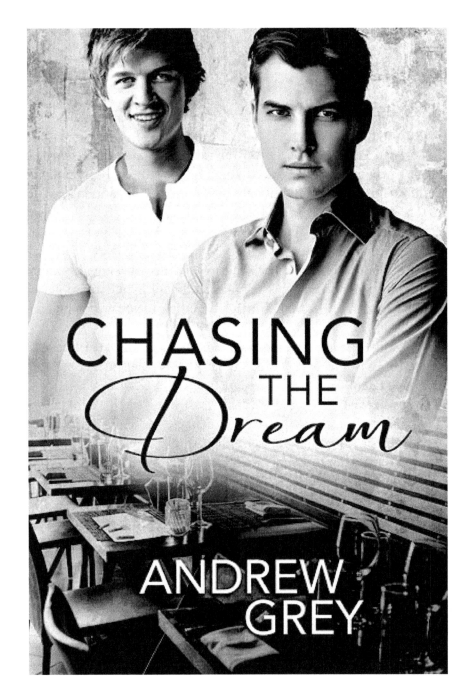

CHASING
THE
Dream

ANDREW
GREY

Born with a silver spoon in his mouth, Brian Paulson has lived a life of luxury and ease. If he's been left lonely because of his family's pursuit of wealth and their own happiness, he figures it's a small price to pay for what he sees as most important: money.

Cade McAllister has never had it easy. He works two jobs to support himself, his mother, and his special-needs brother. They don't have much, but to Cade, love and taking care of the people who are important to him mean more than material possessions. When Cade is mugged in the park, he can't afford to lose what little he has, and he's grateful for Brian's intervention.

Cade is given a chance to return the favor when Brian's grandfather passes away and Brian's assets are frozen. Cade offers Brian a place to stay and helps him find work, and the two men grow closer as they learn the good and the bad of the very different worlds they come from. Just as Brian is starting to see there's more to life than what money can buy, a clause in his grandfather's will could send their relationship up in smoke.

www.dreamspinnerpress.com

EYES
ONLY ME
FOR

ANDREW GREY

For years, Clayton Potter's been friends and workout partners with Ronnie. Though Clay is attracted, he's never come on to Ronnie because, let's face it, Ronnie only dates women.

When Clay's father suffers a heart attack, Ronnie, having recently lost his dad, springs into action, driving Clay to the hospital over a hundred miles away. To stay close to Clay's father, the men share a hotel room near the hospital, but after an emotional day, one thing leads to another, and straight-as-an-arrow Ronnie make a proposal that knocks Clay's socks off! Just a little something to take the edge off.

Clay responds in a way he's never considered. After an amazing night together, Clay expects Ronnie to ignore what happened between them and go back to his old life. Ronnie surprises him and seems interested in additional exploration. Though they're friends, Clay suddenly finds it hard to accept the new Ronnie and suspects that Ronnie will return to his old ways. Maybe they both have a thing or two to learn.

www.dreamspinnerpress.com

DREAMSPUN DESIRES

Andrew Grey

THE LONE RANCHER

He'll do anything to save the ranch, including baring it all.

He'll do anything to save the ranch, including baring it all.

Aubrey Klein is in real trouble—he needs some fast money to save the family ranch. His solution? A weekend job as a stripper at a club in Dallas. For two shows each Saturday, he is the star as The Lone Rancher.

It leads to at least one unexpected revelation: after a show, Garrett Lamston, an old friend from school, approaches the still-masked Aubrey to see about some extra fun… and Aubrey had no idea Garrett was gay. As the two men dodge their mothers' attempts to set them up with girls, their friendship deepens, and one thing leads to another.

Aubrey know his life stretching between the ranch and the club is a house of cards. He just hopes he can keep it standing long enough to save the ranch and launch the life—and the love—he really hopes he can have.

www.dreamspinnerpress.com

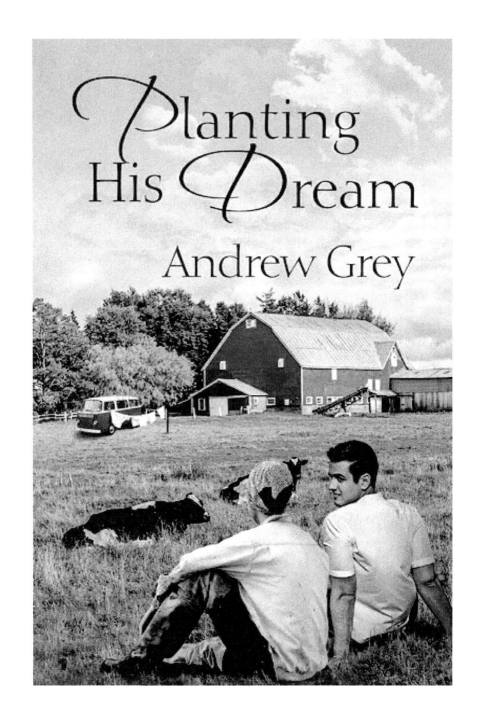

Foster dreams of getting away, but after his father's death, he has to take over the family dairy farm. It soon becomes clear his father hasn't been doing the best job of running it, so not only does Foster need to take over the day-to-day operations, he also needs to find new ways of bringing in revenue.

Javi has no time to dream. He and his family are migrant workers, and daily survival is a struggle, so they travel to anywhere they can get work. When they arrive in their old van, Foster arranges for Javi to help him on the farm.

To Javi's surprise, Foster listens to his ideas and actually puts them into action. Over days that turn into weeks, they grow to like and then care for each other, but they come from two very different worlds, and they both have responsibilities to their families that neither can walk away from. Is it possible for them to discover a dream they can share? Perhaps they can plant their own and nurture it together to see it grow, if their different backgrounds don't separate them forever.

www.dreamspinnerpress.com

REKINDLED FLAME

ANDREW GREY

Firefighter Morgan has worked hard to build a home for himself after a nomadic childhood. When Morgan is called to a fire, he finds the family out front, but their tenant still inside. He rescues Richard Smalley, who turns out to be an old friend he hasn't seen in years and the one person he regretted leaving behind.

Richard has had a hard life. He served in the military, where he lost the use of his legs, and has been struggling to make his way since coming home. Now that he no longer has a place to live, Morgan takes him in, but when someone attempts to set fire to Morgan's house, they both become suspicious and wonder what's going on.

Years ago Morgan was gutted when he moved away, leaving Richard behind, so he's happy to pick things up where they left off. But now that Richard seems to be the target of an arsonist, he may not be the safest person to be around.

www.dreamspinnerpress.com

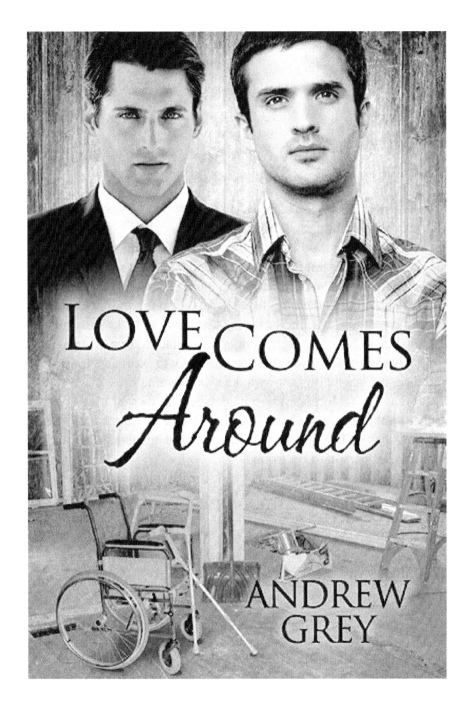

Love Comes Around

Andrew Grey

A Senses Series Story

Artist Arik Bosler is terrified he might have lost his creative gift in the accident that left his hand badly burned. When he's offered the chance to work with renowned artist Ken Brighton, Arik fears his injury will be too much to overcome.

He travels to Pleasanton to meet Ken, where he runs into the intimidating Reg Thompson. Reg, a biker who customizes motorcycles, is a big man with a heart of gold who was rejected by most of his family. Arik is initially afraid of Reg because of his size. However it's Reg's heart that warms Arik's interest and gets him to look past the exterior to let down his guard.

But Arik soon realizes that certain members of Reg's motorcycle club are into things he can't have any part of. Reg can't understand why Arik disappears until he learns Arik's injury was the result of his father's drug activity. Though neither Reg nor Arik wants anything to do with drugs, the new leadership of Reg's club might have other ideas.

www.dreamspinnerpress.com

FOR **MORE** OF THE **BEST** **GAY** ROMANCE

Dreamspinner
PRESS

dreamspinnerpress.com

CPSIA information can be obtained
at www.ICGtesting.com
Printed in the USA
FSOW03n0831070916
24702FS